Hold On

Also from Samantha Young

Hold On

By Samantha Young

A Play On/Big Sky Novella

Introduction by Kristen Proby

EVIL EYE
CONCEPTS

Hold On: A Play On/Big Sky Novella
By Samantha Young
Copyright 2019
ISBN: 978-1-970077-14-8

Published by Evil Eye Concepts, Incorporated

An Introduction to the Kristen Proby Crossover Collection

Everyone knows there's nothing I love more than a happy ending. It's what I do for a living–I'm in LOVE with love. And what's better than love? More love, of course!

Just imagine, Louis Vuitton and Tiffany, collaborating on the world's most perfect handbag. Jimmy Choo and Louboutin, making shoes just for me. Not loving it enough? What if Hugh Grant in *Notting Hill* was the man to barge into Sandra Bullock's office in *The Proposal?* I think we can all agree that Julia Roberts' character would have had her hands full with Ryan Reynolds.

Now imagine what would happen if one of the characters from my Big Sky Series met up with other characters from some of your favorite authors' series. Well, wonder no more because The Kristen Proby Crossover Collection is here, and I could not be more excited!

Rachel Van Dyken, Laura Kaye, Sawyer Bennett, Monica Murphy, Samantha Young, and K.L. Grayson are all bringing their own beloved characters to play – and find their happy endings – in my world. Can you imagine all the love, laughter and shenanigans in store?

I hope you enjoy the journey between worlds!

Love,
Kristen Proby

The Kristen Proby Crossover Collection features a new novel by Kristen Proby and six by some of her favorite writers:

Kristen Proby – Soaring with Fallon
Sawyer Bennett – Wicked Force
KL Grayson – Crazy Imperfect Love
Laura Kaye – Worth Fighting For
Monica Murphy – Nothing Without You
Rachel Van Dyken – All Stars Fall
Samantha Young – Hold On

Acknowledgments from the Author

There is nothing quite like the feeling when an author you admire and respect reaches out and asks you to collaborate. Thank you, Kristen, for trusting me with the beauty of your Big Sky world. I hope Autumn and Gray have done you proud!

Moreover, a massive thank you to Liz Berry for your never-ending well of support and contagious enthusiasm. It's been a pleasure to join the team to collaborate on this fantastic project and I cannot thank you and M.J. enough for making this such a wonderful experience. To everyone who had a hand in bringing HOLD ON and the entire Big Sky crossover together, thank you!

And to the people who are a constant in my world, always there and making life easier for me in your own way, I can never say thank you enough: my fantastic agent, Lauren Abramo, my wonderful PA Ashleen Walker, and my incredibly supportive parents. I'm so grateful for you all.

I can't write this without also thanking my reader group Sam's Clan McBookish. You always brighten up my day. It means so much to me. Thank you.

And finally, the biggest thank you of all to you, my reader. You are my sunshine.

Sign up for the 1001 Dark Nights Newsletter
and be entered to win a Tiffany Lock necklace.

There's a contest every quarter!

Go to www.1001DarkNights.com to subscribe.

As a bonus, all subscribers can download
FIVE FREE exclusive books!

Chapter One

Whitetail Mountain, Montana
February

The fresh, cold air stung my cheeks as I stared down the snowy slope through my ski goggles.

"Bloody Nora," I muttered under my breath, watching mostly kids skiing on what they called the Bunny Hill. There were a few adult beginners but they were with ski instructors.

"You should go out with an instructor," Catie had said a mere twenty minutes ago, seeming concerned as we strapped on our boots at the rental just across from the lodge.

I'd seen the young instructors, probably college kids making a few extra dollars during the ski season, and they seemed perfectly competent. However, beneath my laidback façade was a great deal of stubbornness and I believed I could do this alone.

It wasn't like I hadn't skied before.

I had.

I'd also broken my leg the last time I'd strapped on a pair of skis.

"Bloody Nora," I repeated.

What was I doing here?

Not here in Montana—*here*. I only had to lift my gaze over the snowy mountains to know why anyone would want to visit Whitetail Mountain. I meant, what the hell was I doing *here*? *Here* in snow boots clicked into the skis, wearing goggles, a hat, thick gloves, and an admittedly adorable emerald green snow suit I couldn't resist buying.

Because what I really wanted to do was go back to the lodge and wait for my afternoon spa appointments to begin. I wanted to lounge by the pool with a glass of wine and write down my life plan. That's what I was here for. To get some space from my life back in Glasgow and "find myself" in the snowy hills of Montana. Like a heroine in a Reese Witherspoon movie. Just me and my thoughts. And the occasional third wheeling of Catie and her husband Kyle's annual holiday.

My friend and her hubby were currently on the top slopes as they were experienced skiers.

"Face your fears, Autumn," Kyle had said before we got on the chairlift that would drop me on the Bunny Hill.

Face my fears. Yes, I knew that's what this moment was *supposed* to symbolize.

When I was fourteen I'd broken my leg on a high school skiing trip and I'd vowed never to get on skis again. But this year had been rough and I'd grown increasingly afraid of facing the fact that I was floundering in life. Strapping on a pair of skis was supposed to help me face those fears. If I could ski again, I could get my life back in order.

But...

"What utter rubbish," I huffed.

Skiing was rubbish! I hated it. You only faced a fear if it was going to make your life better. How was skiing going to make my life better?

A massage.

A massage would make my life infinitely better.

Decided, I pulled my ski poles out of the snow with a little too much vigor and immediately threw my weight off balance, my skis flying out from under me.

"Oh...oh..." I tried to right my center of gravity but threw myself too far forward. "Oh sh—" Suddenly I was heading down the slope! And I was heading for a woman and a ski instructor and I couldn't remember how to stop.

"Out of the way!" I warned.

The ski instructor, his expression masked by snow sunglasses, looked up at me and then, instead of getting out of my way, got deliberately in it.

I smacked straight into his large body, winding myself and knocking him off his skis, taking him to the snow.

"Oof!" he grunted, sounding more than a little bit winded himself.

Mortified, I tried to clamber off him. Unfortunately, my knee connected somewhere it shouldn't.

"Fuck," he wheezed.

"I'm so sorry, I'm so sorry." Somehow I got off him without causing him any further injury and righted myself on my skis as he curled into a fetal position in the snow. "Are you okay?"

He waved me off, apparently unable to speak.

I looked at the woman who hovered over him, wincing. "Is he okay?"

She shot me a dirty look. "Does he look okay? If you can't ski, you shouldn't be out here without an instructor."

"I was trying to leave. I slipped and lost control..." I looked back down at the instructor who was taking his time getting up onto his skis. He braced his hands on his knees for a moment and then straightened, his lips pinched together in pain.

It was then I realized how big he was. And even without being able to see his eyes because they were covered by snow sunglasses, I could tell he was quite a bit older than the rest of the boy-men instructors. "Are you all right?"

"I will be." He put his hands to his hips as I looked up at him. I was tall for a woman at five foot nine but this guy was just *tall*. He had to be at least six foot three. And broad shouldered.

Big guy.

And I'd just kneed him in the junk.

Gulp.

"What the hell are you doing on the slope without an instructor?" he groused in an attractively rough American accent.

"Trying to leave. What the hell were you doing deliberately putting yourself in my path? I told you to get out of the way. So, you know, your injury is really your own fault."

His jaw grew taut a second before he retorted, "You hadn't had time to build up much momentum but if I let you go flying down the slope you could have collided with another guest and caused them injury and whatever happened *you* would have gotten hurt. So you're welcome."

Feeling foolish but annoyed by his condescending tone, I didn't offer thanks. Instead, I felt a little petulant. "I said I'm sorry."

"Get your ass off the slopes and sign up for an instructor." He jerked his chin, indicating behind me where the chair lift was. I noted that he had a very strong jawline. With stubble. Nice lips, too. "I'm all booked today but they'll slide you in if I get a cancellation. Just ask for Grayson King."

"No, thank you, Mr. King," I replied. "Sorry again." I turned to leave, throwing the scowling woman an apologetic smile.

"No thank you?"

I glanced back over my shoulder at his tone.

He sounded annoyed.

Very annoyed.

Oh no.

"No thank you?" he repeated. "You're seriously going to come back out here without instruction?"

"No. I have no intention of coming back out here *at all.*" I threw an arm out to indicate the expanse of the slopes and my skis slid again. "Ah!" I righted myself, this time not sliding. My heart pounded in my ears. "Oh thank Christ! Aye, okay. Right. I'm heading in before I or someone else suffers serious injury."

"Yeah, you do that."

He still sounded irritated.

Dear God, how many times did I need to apologize? "I will!" I threw back over my shoulder, letting him know that now *he* was annoying *me.* "Apparently apologies aren't enough," I muttered under my breath. "Didn't even want to come on this stupid slope and then I fall but does anyone ask if I'm okay? No. Where's the bloody spa when you need it?"

"Try not to take anyone else out." If I wasn't mistaken he now sounded as though he were amused.

Now he was laughing at me? My cheeks burned. Him being angry was much better than him laughing at me.

I dug my poles into the snow and hoofed it further up the slope. The distance allowed me some bravery. "You better remember to nurse your manhood, Mr. King!" I reminded him about his recent painful injury.

"You nursing it for me sounds better!"

My lips parted on a huff and I looked back over my shoulder in outrage.

Even from a distance I could see him grinning at me.

"There are children in the vicinity!"

"You're the one that mentioned it!"

Dammit, I was. Muttering under my breath again I made my way back up the slope to the chairlift and looked anywhere but at Grayson King.

Well, this trip was going super well so far.

* * * *

"Hey, sweetheart." My big brother's voice was a welcome sound as I sat on the end of my bed and stared out over the miraculous vista.

I was independently wealthy and I hated why.

It did mean, however, being able to afford a stunning suite on the top floor of the Snow Ghost Lodge. My hotel suite not only had a huge four poster bed, a sitting area with a gas fire, and a massive, luxurious bathroom with a roll-top bath tub, it had floor-to-ceiling windows that looked out over the valley. I could see the town of Cunningham Falls and the lake from here.

Just wow.

Between that and Killian's voice in my ear I was feeling much, much better than I had been an hour ago.

"You're home then?" I said.

"Safe and sound. Skylar's crashed out or I'd let you say hi."

"No, let her sleep." I would have liked to say hello but I knew for a fact that my brother's girlfriend needed rest. The last two years of her life had been crazy, the last few months even more so, and the last week, intense.

Skylar Finch used to be the lead singer of a hugely successful pop-rock band called Tellurian. Skylar became tabloid fodder pretty quickly, mostly because of an on-again off-again relationship she had with her guitarist. She'd hated the fame and she'd hated their toxic relationship. To hide her unhappiness from her mum—the person she loved best in the whole world—because she felt she owed her mum for all the sacrifices she'd made for Skylar, she'd pushed her away. And then her mum and stepdad were victims of a highly publicized burglary that ended in their murder. Skylar left the band and disappeared off the map. Until Killian, my big brother and label executive, found her in our home city of Glasgow. She was busking and homeless. We helped her get her life back together. Because of our own less than idyllic upbringing, Killian was pretty closed off emotionally. At that point the only person he let in was me. So when I saw him and Skylar falling for each other, I was worried he was going to royally screw it up.

He almost did.

But my big brother loves Skylar Finch. And I mean he loves her in a way I didn't know existed outside of movies and romance novels. And she loves him with the same intensity. I adore that for Sky because she's special and she deserves happiness after everything she's been through. But I love it for Killian more.

When the paparazzi found Skylar a few months ago things were crazy! But they settled down somewhat and the three of us had a lovely Christmas together. And then Killian and I accompanied Skylar to Los Angeles to see her ex-bandmates and tie up some professional and financial stuff. We'd then stood by her side when she returned to her hometown of Billings in Montana so she could visit her mum's grave.

It had been a tough and extremely emotional time but I was glad we could be there for her.

Afterward, they headed back to Scotland and I travelled to Whitetail Mountain to hang out with Catie and Kyle.

"You get to the lodge okay?"

I had. Even though I'd been a little nervous (okay, a lot!) as the commuter bus drove up Whitetail Mountain. It was well paved and sanded but there were these treacherous, narrow hairpin turns that they called switchbacks here and I'd felt my whole body tense as we wound up the mountain. However, I was not tense enough to miss the view or the cute B&B we passed called The Hideout, thinking I would have liked to have stayed there. But when the bus drove into the snow village where the lodge was located I realized why Catie and Kyle holidayed at the Snow Ghost every year.

I could see ski lifts on their climb to the summit, the snow-covered evergreens, a building complex that looked like it housed rental apartments.

There was a ski rental shop and a café, as well as a few little independent stores.

The bus had parked in a lot before a beautiful lodge that somehow managed to be grand and rustic at the same time. The Snow Ghost Lodge.

I loved the name. As soon as Catie sent me the lodge website link so I could book a room, I fell in love. The lodge sat right at the base of the ski lifts so guests could shimmy out on their skis and set off right away.

"Yes, and I think this might be what heaven looks like," I replied.

"I was worried about you going up that mountain."

I wasn't going to tell my brother I had been, too. "Well I'm fine. Although decidedly not going to ski."

"Why not?"

I told him what happened and then had to wait for a few minutes for him to stop laughing. It was nice to hear my big brother laugh, just not at my expense. "Are you done?"

"Only you"—his voice still trembled with amusement— "could knock a man off his feet and knee him in the 'nads within seconds of hitting the slopes."

"Hey, I'm usually very graceful."

"Until there's snow."

"I broke my leg *once*. One time!"

"Aye, skiing. What about two winters ago when you took out three people in the supermarket car park when you slipped on ice and fell into a load of trolleys?"

"I could have killed someone, Killian. That's not a funny story."

"I just don't understand how someone who dances like an angel suddenly has no grace whatsoever when white cold stuff hits the ground."

I glared at my view. "You could have reminded me of this when I told you I was planning on coming here."

"Why? You need time for yourself. I'm glad you're out there. But for my peace of mind… promise me, no more skiing."

"I'll stick to the spa."

"Thank you."

"You must be tired. I'll let you go."

"Okay. Check in with me tomorrow."

I rolled my eyes at his protectiveness. "Or the next day."

"No, tomorrow, Autumn."

Hearing the sternness in his voice I nodded and then remembered he couldn't see me. "Tomorrow."

"Right. Off to bed. Night, sweetheart."

"Night, big brother."

"Autumn."

Something about his tone made me tense as I replied, "Yes?"

"You know I love you, right?"

Tears pricked my eyes. I knew my brother loved me. He'd spent his life raising me, protecting me, and making sure I didn't feel the sting of my uncle's lack of affection. When I was little, Killian told me he loved me all the time but as we'd gotten older, he'd stopped saying the words. His actions always spoke louder than them anyway. That didn't mean they didn't feel beautiful. And I had Skylar to thank for them.

"Always. I love you, too."

After we hung up I stared out at the view for a while, feeling momentarily content. Momentarily because I knew that it wouldn't last. I was restless deep down in my soul and growing more so.

The alarm on my phone went off to let me know my first spa treatment was up. I'd booked a whole bunch of treatments before even arriving so I wouldn't miss out but after my disastrous morning on the slopes I'd checked at reception to see if they had any availability for other treatments.

An Indian head massage appointment was available.

Hell yes!

I made my way down to the spa in my bikini and fluffy white robe from the room. I also wore the complimentary slippers and had a towel rolled up under my arm. The spa was on the floor below mine which made sense when you saw it—the spa took advantage of the views. I saw on the website that there was an outdoor heated infinity pool that jutted out over the mountains. I couldn't wait to try it out.

But first up, head massage.

I loved spas.

I loved the pampering from the moment you entered. I loved the smell of aromatherapy and chlorine from the pool. I loved the misty condensation in the air from the steam room and sauna.

I loved getting a massage.

I loved that when you were there you didn't have to think about anything but relaxing.

I *loved* spas and was definitely more of a spa girl than a ski girl.

After handing me a glass of champagne topped with orange juice, a friendly woman named Cora led me through the reception area to the indoor pool. Tranquil music played softly in the background as she guided me to a reserved lounger by the pool.

"Your therapist is Adrienne and she'll be with you soon," Cora said and left me to it.

Instead of planning my life like I'd intended to while I waited for my masseuse, I laid back on my lounger, closed my eyes, and drifted off.

I was here for ten days.

That was plenty of time to plan my life.

For now a day at the spa *was* my life plan.

Chapter Two

By the time I'd made my way back up to my room after my treatments I was more relaxed than I remembered being in a long time. I wasn't back in my room five minutes when Catie texted to tell me I was meeting her and Kyle for a romantic dinner for three in an hour. When Catie asked me to come with them on this trip, I knew she'd extended the invitation because she was worried about me. She thought I needed a break from life and since she and Kyle never relaxed more than they did on Whitetail Mountain, she thought the place would work wonders for me.

I agreed because why not? But now that I was here, I was concerned about cramping their style and worried Catie and Kyle hadn't thought about how having me along would interrupt their much-needed alone time.

Before I could text back to tell her I had other plans for the evening she texted again.

We want you there. No excuses. Dinner. An hour. Don't make me haul my arse up to your fancy suite Xx

I laughed because my friend knew me so well and also because she'd been jokingly grumbling about my suite since I booked it. She and Kyle had a standard room a few floors below me but I knew she didn't really care I was in a suite. Catie just loved to tease me whenever the opportunity arose.

Wouldn't dream of it. See you in an hour. Xx

The restaurant in the lodge was pretty nice. Catie told me the food was great and that locals booked tables there for special occasions so it was always busy. I was that girl that looked semi-dressed up no matter the event because I adored fashion and high heels. That night I decided on a high-waist forest green pencil skirt and a dark gold silk top with short art deco beaded sleeves that draped delicately over my shoulders; it showed lots of collarbone and a hint of cleavage. When I tucked the top into the skirt the whole ensemble accentuated my curves. I added gold strappy sandals, decided against jewelry, and wore my long auburn hair how I normally wore it: down in beachy waves that almost touched my lower back.

Grabbing the forest green clutch I'd bought with the skirt, I gave myself one more look in the mirror. Pencil skirts were so on trend right now. Usually Italian designers had them in their shows every year but they were on runways all over the globe this year and I for one loved they'd made a big comeback. There was nothing more flattering than a pencil skirt.

Not caring if I was overly dressed up because that was just me, I strode out of my room wondering if I should add "something in fashion" to my list of possible career options. I'd enjoyed shopping for Skylar when she first started working with my brother. Killian had worried I'd force my style onto her when he asked me to buy her new clothes but I found I gauged her personal style pretty well and was able to advise her accordingly. Once we helped her gain weight and get healthy again, I took her shopping, Skylar always looked tricked out. She managed to be sexy, alternative rocker girl whether she was in jeans and a tee or a tight black dress. But that was just Skylar. The woman exuded an undeniable amount of charisma that you were either born with or you just didn't have. She had it. And it was one of the reasons the paparazzi and her fans were so obsessed with her.

I couldn't take credit for that but I could take credit for some of the really cute items in her current wardrobe.

Stylist? Hmm. I'd put that on the list even though it sounded incredibly unrealistic. It would be a fun career though. Or maybe I'd get bored.

Och, I didn't know.

I'd think about it in the morning because it would only stress me out before dinner.

The restaurant was on the same floor as my suite so it didn't take me long to wander down the corridor to it. When I got there Catie and Kyle still hadn't arrived so the host led me to the bar, where I slipped onto a stool to wait for them. I gazed around the restaurant. It had a modern, rustic vibe that I liked and as Catie had already warned me, was packed with people. She and Kyle had booked us a table for dinner every night before our arrival but I wasn't planning on joining them every night. They needed alone time at some point. And although I could see larger groups dining out together there was a really romantic feel about the place. There were tealights on every table and white fairy lights scattered through large potted topiaries that were placed strategically throughout. Not overdone. Just right. Still, between the soft lighting and the huge, wide windows at the back of the restaurant that provided a fabulous view over the ski hill, it was definitely a perfect place to be with someone you wanted to play footsie with under the table.

"What can I get you?"

I turned at the male voice and found the bartender, a guy around my age, smiling at me. "Oh. A glass of your house red, please."

"Well, I'd know that Scottish accent anywhere," a deep, familiar voice said behind me and I turned slightly on my stool and felt my stomach dip as the most beautiful man I'd ever seen in my life slid onto the stool next to mine.

Even though I hadn't seen all of his face this morning I knew who he was.

Grayson King. The instructor I'd kneed in the 'nads.

Oh my God.

Holy Moly...

And now I was staring.

But in all fairness he was staring intensely back at me and with the most delicious blue eyes. He had thick dark brown hair that he left just long enough to curl at the nape of his neck.

Then there were those eyes. A rich cobalt blue framed with not long but thick, black lashes.

As for his face with his cut cheekbones, wide, square jaw, and full mouth, he was the picture of masculine beauty. If it weren't for the slight crook in his nose that suggested it had been broken at some point, his unshaven face, and his imposing build, he might have been too perfect.

But he wasn't. He was gorgeous with an edge. He had faint laughter lines around his eyes and I guessed him at around my brother's age—about thirty years old or so. He wore a black dress shirt open at the collar and black suit trousers. There was no part of his outfit that said "I'm trying" and he looked effortlessly hot.

Between his immense attractiveness and the fact that I'd embarrassed myself in front of him I felt unusually defensive. "May I help you?"

He seemed not in the least perturbed by my tone. Instead he turned to the bartender. "A red for the lady, a beer for me."

"You got it." The bartender wandered off to do as bid.

Grayson's lips curled up at the corners as he angled his body toward mine. "You're the girl who flattened me today."

"One, I'm a woman, not a girl."

His lids lowered as his gaze dipped down my body and leisurely back up again in a way that forced me to hide a shiver of desire.

What. The. Hell.

"Two"—I was pretty sure my voice now sounded hoarse—"I don't weigh enough to *flatten* you. Have you seen you?"

When he returned his gaze to my eyes there was a heat in his he didn't bother hiding. "You're right. Poor choice of words."

Unsure how to deal with his blatant interest considering he was the sexiest man I'd ever met and I definitely had not come to Montana for a fling, I willed the bartender to come back.

In fact, I willed Catie and Kyle to hurry the heck up.

"I don't get it," Grayson said.

"Get what?"

"I was around the other side of the bar, saw you walk in. Didn't know you were the *woman* from today. You glide across the restaurant in a pair of sky-high heels like you're barefooted. No way, you walking in here with all that grace, I'd know you were the woman that took me out on the slopes today."

My cheeks burned, not only at his compliment but at his teasing. "I'm not good on skis," I replied through gritted teeth.

"Oh, I got that." He grinned.

God, even his grin, slightly crooked like his nose, was bloody sexy. *Not fair, Universe!* My staring at him like an idiot made his smile disappear. His eyes narrowed slightly. "You waiting on someone?"

"Yes," I answered honestly, even though I suspected he was asking if I was waiting on a man.

His gaze fell to my left hand and I knew he was looking for a ring. When he found none our eyes locked again. His expression was altogether too soft and too hot. "What's your name, angel?"

I didn't know why I gave it to him. I shouldn't have. "Autumn."

His lips parted as he studied my face and hair. Voice hoarse, he said, "Fuck, that's perfect."

There was something almost reverent in his tone that made my spine straighten. "And you're Grayson?"

"You can call me Gray."

The bartender returned. "Wine. Beer."

"My tab," Gray replied as he gently pushed the wine toward me and took his beer.

"Oh no, I'll pay for my own drink."

"No way." Gray shook his head at the bartender and the guy walked off to serve someone else.

I stared at my wine, uncertain if it came with a whole bunch of strings attached to it.

"It's just a drink, Autumn."

"I'm not…" I looked him directly in the eyes. "I'm not here to hook up or get involved with anyone."

"You got a man?"

"No. And I'm not looking for one."

Gray leaned into me and I got a whiff of delicious, spicy, musky, masculine cologne that made me want to press my face into his throat.

Fuck.

"Take the drink."

"No strings attached to it, right?" I curled my fingers around the stem of the wineglass.

Those blue eyes held me utterly captive as he replied, "Woman, you're the most beautiful fucking thing I've ever seen in my life. Take the drink or leave the drink, I'm not going anywhere until you say you'll have dinner with me."

My breath caught at the epic compliment. He sounded so sincere I wanted to believe him. Yet, he wasn't the first man to tell me I was beautiful (although admittedly he was the first to say it like that!) and I somehow always ended up getting hurt after it got them what they wanted.

"I can't." Even I heard how unsure I sounded.

"You have to." He gave me a teasing smile. "Or I'm going to pine. I'm going to pine *hard.*"

God, what a charmer. I shook my head, smiling despite myself. "You're good with a line."

Suddenly I felt the rough calluses on his palm as he circled my wrist with his hand and gave me a gentle squeeze. "Not feeding you a line here, angel." He let go but trailed his fingers across the top of my arm before doing so. Goosebumps rose up all over my skin as I imagined him touching me elsewhere. My breath stuttered and, as if he knew the lustful territory my thoughts had wandered into, his eyes darkened.

"Fuck," he huffed, seeming just as stunned by the attraction between us as I was.

"There you are!"

At the sound of Catie's voice, I sagged with relief.

Relief because holding this attraction back was *not* easy. And we'd just freaking met!

Suddenly Catie and Kyle were there. Kyle stared at Gray with an assessing expression. Catie stared at him like he was a movie star.

And I rudely got up without introducing them. "Our table is ready?"

"Uh..." Catie tore her gaze from Gray. "Yes."

"Then let's eat. I'm hungry." I gently pushed her away from the bar, and Kyle, who seemed to read my expression, helped me out by physically turning her around. I looked back at Gray as Kyle guided Catie to our table. "It was nice to meet you. Apologies again for today on the slopes."

He shook his head at me. "Going to need a different kind of apology."

I gave him a regretful smile because he was charming and for some bizarre reason I didn't want him to think I was an aloof cow immune to that charm. "I'm afraid it's the only kind I have in me to give."

Before he could say anything else that might make me wish things were different I hurried across the restaurant to my friends.

Part of me was really pissed off I'd met Grayson King. But a bigger part of me was pissed off that I'd met him *now*. Pre-Darren I might have let Gray buy me a drink. I might have even let him come back to my room for a fling in the snowy mountains of Montana. Although I wasn't anti-men, I was just anti-men *for now* until I got my shit together. After what I'd been through in my previous relationship no one would blame me for giving up on men entirely, but I wasn't the type to give up hope so easily. I was an optimist. I still believed the love of my life was out there somewhere. Someone who would treat me the way Killian treated Skylar.

However, now was definitely not the time in my life to be looking for that. Especially not with some guy who lived an ocean away. Plus it was crazy to even consider that the feeling between me and Grayson King was more than just animal attraction.

"Okay, so who is that?" Catie asked as soon as I took my seat.

I snuck a peek at Gray sitting at the bar, staring down at the beer in his hand as if deep in thought. God, he was so freaking handsome.

"A ski instructor. I accidentally collided with him on the slopes today."

"He is bloody gorgeous," Catie said all wide-eyed and dreamy. She smiled apologetically at her husband. "Sorry, babe, just stating a fact."

Kyle made a face and then turned to me. "He bothering you?"

"Of course he wasn't bothering her," Catie replied before I could. "That man is never bothering a woman."

I chuckled. "Oh you know him, do you?"

"I know there's not a woman alive who wouldn't want him bothering her."

"Well, you found her," I retorted. "I'm not here for that. You know I'm not."

She suddenly winced and I knew I'd reminded her of Darren. "Of course. Sorry, babe."

"Nothing to be sorry for. If things were different he is definitely a man I'd..." I trailed off as I looked beyond my friend's shoulder and saw Gray move away from the bar to join a very attractive woman. Disappointment settled in my gut as I realized he really *had* been feeding me a line.

"Player," Kyle muttered, sounding pissed off and I dragged my gaze from Gray to find Kyle glaring in his direction.

"What?" Catie asked, about to turn around.

I hissed, "Don't look."

Kyle explained, "He was chatting up our girl, all the while waiting on his date."

For some stupid reason it hurt.

I didn't even know him but I felt this burning pang in my chest.

"Woman, you're the most beautiful fucking thing I've ever seen in my life."

I'd believed him. I'd stupidly, deep down, believed him.

"That doesn't mean anything," Catie said. "He was probably sitting waiting on his date and took one look at you and forgot about her." She gestured to me. "It's the Autumn Factor."

Despite my disappointment, I smiled. "The Autumn Factor?"

"Aye, the Autumn Factor. You walk into a room and everybody forgets whatever the hell they're doing. It happened to me when we met at college."

"Oh, do go on." Kyle crossed his arms and leaned them on the table with a teasing smirk.

Catie rolled her eyes. "Not in a sexy way, you perv. I had just never seen a girl as beautiful as Autumn in real life before."

I felt my cheeks heat because I was terribly British and never knew how to deal with compliments. At five foot nine, I was tall, slender but with hips, an arse, and I wore a C-cup bra. My hair was a rich red-gold auburn and my favorite thing about myself. I got my hair from my dad. Killian had a different father so he had dark hair but we both got our dark brown eyes from our mum. We also were both gifted with her long, thick lashes. But while Killian had his dad's slightly olive skin tone that made him look tan all year round, I got my dad's pale skin. Alabaster and not prone to blemish. It was good skin. Plus nature had seen fit to give me my mother's full heart-shaped lips.

I didn't have any hang-ups about my physical appearance. In a way that I hoped wasn't arrogant or conceited, I was content with what I saw in the mirror. But sometimes it made me uncomfortable when people fixated on my looks because it was either what drew them toward me or pushed them away from me. I'd been bullied pretty badly in high school and when Killian eventually found out, I couldn't do a thing to stop him from tracking the ringleader down. Whatever he said put the fear of God into her because she never bothered me again. But Killian had said after a mere conversation with her, he had known she'd come after me because I was beautiful, and, for whatever reason, that made her insecure and jealous.

Thankfully, I had not made Catie insecure. I remembered how she walked right up to me when I entered the library that day and told me I had "bloody awesome hair."

I'd loved her immediately.

"Well, Catie, babe, you might be right," Kyle suddenly muttered and threw me a look. "He's staring over here and making no qualms about it in front of the girl he's with."

I stiffened at this news and couldn't stop my gaze from flying over Catie's shoulder to search Gray out.

I found him just four tables away, his companion's back to us, so he was directly in my line of sight. And he *was* looking at me. In an intense way that made me shiver.

I looked down at my menu. "That's a little rude."

"Oh, girl he's with just followed his gaze. She's spotted you and she doesn't look happy."

"Would you if you were on a date with someone who was staring at someone else?" I felt a blush hit my cheeks. There was no denying I liked that a man as charismatic as Grayson King liked what he saw when he looked at me, but if he could treat his date with unforgiveable rudeness then he could treat me the same way. "Just ignore him."

However, as we ordered and then started to make our way through our meal I felt Gray's attention still burning on me. Like I had no control over my gaze, it unwillingly searched for his, our eyes colliding again and again across the restaurant. I squirmed uncomfortably until halfway through the meal I heard the squeal of a chair sliding across wood. My eyes flew in the direction of the sound and widened as I saw the brunette with Gray march away from the table. When I looked back at him he turned from watching her walk away and gave me a casual shrug.

I glared at him.

He smirked.

"Guess she got sick of not having his attention," Kyle snorted.

"It's not funny. He's rude."

"Do you know what's really not funny?" Catie huffed. "Having my back to the fecking entertainment!"

Kyle burst out laughing but I couldn't. I was upset that Gray could treat someone so callously and even more upset that I could be this upset over someone I'd just met.

Thankfully I felt the heat of his stare disappear and watched as he walked out of the restaurant. I ignored how the sight of his tall, powerful body gave me flutters low in my belly.

"Let's just enjoy dinner," I said.

And for the most part we did, even though we all knew I was stupidly distracted.

"Drinks?" Catie asked as we left the table after finishing up.

"You two stay." My friends should have some alone time. "I'm tired."

Kyle studied me. "You sure?"

I smiled to reassure them. "Yes. Have a good night. I'll see you tomorrow."

Much shorter than me at five foot three (five foot seven in heels) Catie went up on her tip toes to kiss my cheek. "Night, babe."

"Night, sweetie."

Next Kyle kissed my cheek and I squeezed his shoulder. "Thanks for a lovely night."

He grinned at me, completely aware that it had been a discombobulating evening for me. "Night, Autumn."

I left them at the bar, strolling out of the restaurant, thinking I might just go straight to bed and try to sleep away the strange events of the day. Looking at my feet, or my fabulous shoes really, as I walked out into the hallway that would lead me back to my room, I would have missed him if he hadn't said my name.

I stumbled to a stop and glanced to my right to see Gray leaning against the wall outside of the restaurant. Waiting on me?

He pushed off the wall and strolled toward me. A teasing smirk played around his mouth as he stepped right into my personal space. I wanted to step back but didn't want to give him the satisfaction of knowing his nearness affected me.

In my sandals I was almost the same height as him but he was so broad-shouldered he still managed to make me feel delicate and feminine. I hated how much I loved that. "What are you doing here?"

"Let me give you a lesson tomorrow," he replied.

I blinked, having not expected that. "I don't want to learn to ski."

"Then let me buy you dinner tomorrow night so I can change your mind."

I thought of the brunette and scowled. "I've seen how you treat your dinner companions, so no, thank you."

Gray's eyebrows drew together in a much more effective scowl than mine. "She's here on a bachelorette trip. She's the bride."

My lips parted in surprise at this information.

"Yeah." His mouth twisted in disdain. "She's the woman who was on the slopes with me today and she told me straight up she wanted one last fling before she got married. I didn't say shit to that and obviously she was expecting me to jump on it. So when I didn't give her what she wanted in private, she asked me to dinner in front of all her girls and I didn't want to humiliate her. I saw no harm in dinner but had no intention of going beyond that. I didn't know you'd walk in there tonight, so I had no way of knowing I'd spend the whole fucking thing distracted by a redhead who I'm not afraid to admit has knocked me on my ass. Let me take you to dinner."

I wanted to believe him. I really, really wanted to believe him. And everything he said was good. More than good. I think I did believe him about the snow bunny but I wasn't sure about the rest. And the timing… oh God, the timing was bad.

And why did he have to be standing so close? So close I could smell him, I could feel the heat of him, and I really, really wanted to slide my hand over his chest and see if his pecs were as hard as they looked.

Damn, damn, damn.

I yanked my gaze from his because I was drowning in it. "I'm not here to meet anyone. I'm sorry."

"I'd maybe believe that if you'd look at me when you say it."

Hearing the amusement in his voice I did look at him. I glowered. "When I look at you, you make me want to say yes!"

Gray grinned. Huge. "That's not a bad thing, angel."

"It is to me." I stepped back. "Now good night."

He moved to block my escape. "Breakfast?"

I stifled a smile at his persistence and shook my head.

"Lunch?"

My traitorous lips twitched. "No, I'm sorry."

He cocked his head to the side to study me. "You know even you telling me 'no' sounds like heaven to my ears. I could listen to you talk in that sexy as fuck accent for the rest of my life."

I gave a huff of disbelieving laughter. "What a line."

"It's not a line." He stepped back into my personal space. "Have dinner with me."

My gaze dropped to his mouth and I whispered, "No."

"You can't stare at my mouth like that and expect me to believe that no."

I wrenched my eyes back to his. "Gray, we can't do this. It's a firm no."

"Well, I'm just going to ask you again tomorrow."

Exasperated, I stepped around him before he could stop me. "I'm going to take a wild guess and say harassing guests is against hotel policy."

Gray turned with me. "Oh, this isn't harassment. This is seeing something I want more than I've ever wanted anything and doing what I can to get it."

Shocked, I replied breathily, "That's insane. You don't even know me."

He shrugged and said seriously (*very seriously*), "I took one look in those gorgeous brown eyes of yours and knew I'd do anything to get to know you. I need to take you out to do that so… are you going to help me out here and say yes?"

My heart was pounding like crazy and I had absolutely no idea why. What was it about this guy that affected me so much? And why did it feel dangerous and thrilling at the same bloody time?

"Autumn?"

I shook my head. "If you're looking to get laid there's a snow bunny who made it clear she'd give you that."

"I don't screw other men's women and even if I did, I don't want her. She doesn't make my blood hot."

My eyes widened. Was he alluding that I *did* make his blood hot? "I'm not anyone's casual fuck, Gray."

His eyes darkened. "I got that, angel, the second you strutted that fine ass through the restaurant. That's not what this is about. Although for the record, you saying the word 'fuck' when you're actually talking about 'fucking' in that sweet voice of yours… not going to lie." He grinned. "You *definitely* make my blood hot."

I blushed. I freaking blushed!

Gray laughed. "Oh that's just making it worse."

"Stop it!" I huffed, covering my cheeks with my hands.

"Jesus, you're adorable. Didn't know that was possible."

"What?"

"Sexy, beautiful, and adorable. The trifecta of perfect."

I smiled but said, "No one's perfect, Gray."

"No, they're not so give me a break here. Let me get to know you so I can find out for myself that you're not perfect. Otherwise I'm going to pine my life away."

He somehow managed to strike a perfect balance between smooth and coarse charm that seriously worked for me. *Damn it.* I sighed. "Fine. Ask me again tomorrow."

"Or you could just say yes now," he pushed. I gave him a look and he grinned. "Fine. I'll ask you tomorrow."

Finally, I made myself walk away. But I'd only taken a few steps when he said, "Nice skirt by the way."

Meaning he was watching my ass.

I turned to look over my shoulder and rolled my eyes before strutting off.

His answering laughter made me smile all the way back to my suite.

Chapter Three

The next morning I was a little tired because thoughts of Gray kept whirling around my mind. A lot of them sexy thoughts. I missed breakfast with Catie and Kyle so they were already heading out to the slopes by the time I dragged my arse out of the shower.

Grabbing my ereader, I headed downstairs to the reception to double check the times for my manicure and pedicure appointments. Jeanette, the woman manning the desk, was so helpful and didn't even blink when I asked her if there was a slot available for more treatments toward the end of my stay. I intended to use the hell out of that spa.

The reception area of the Snow Ghost Lodge was wonderful. As soon as I entered the building, it felt like I'd walked into a mountain retreat. To the left of the entrance was a large river-rock fireplace where a healthy fire snapped and crackled in a way that invited me toward it. There were comfortable couches and chairs near the fire for guests to warm up and opposite that was a table with cookies and warm cider I could help myself to. I considered curling up on one of the couches to read but I really needed my morning coffee.

So I found myself eating breakfast pastries in the coffeehouse across from the lodge while I sipped at an Americano and read. I was deep into my book so it took me a second to realize someone had taken the other seat at my bistro table.

I looked up from my ebook and my heart thumped hard in my

chest at the sight of Gray. This was followed by a flutter of butterflies that shocked the heck out of me since the last time I could remember having butterflies over a guy was when I was thirteen and still dancing ballet. I'd gone to a ballet "summer camp" of sorts in London to prepare for my audition at RSC (The Royal Conservatoire of Scotland). There I'd met Mikhail, a fourteen-year-old Russian dancer, who was superb, brooding and beautiful. He'd been my first kiss.

Butterflies. Wow. I didn't think a grown woman could still get those.

Oh boy, was I in trouble.

Gray wore a small smile as he studied me. I noted he was in a warm jacket and jeans, like me, and not in full snow gear. He still hadn't shaved.

Yum.

"You want to finish that coffee and meet me on the slopes?"

I shook my head. "I'm not skiing. I hate skiing. What are you doing here? Don't you have work to do?"

"Nope." His gaze dipped to my ereader. "What are you reading?"

"The Devil in Winter."

He chuckled. "Is that a joke?"

I couldn't help but smile. The man made me want to smile all the time. What was that? "It's not actually. Just ironic. It's an historical romance. My favorite book."

For some reason this made him grin. "Your favorite book, huh? See, now I'm getting somewhere."

"I also told you I hate skiing," I reminded him for some bizarre reason. I shouldn't encourage the flirt, something I'd decided this morning after a night's rest. As much as I was inexplicably drawn to this man, the whole reason I'd come to Montana was because people (mostly boyfriends) had tried to take advantage of me my whole life. I wanted to be the open person I was but I didn't want to be vulnerable. I had to toughen up and find out who I was before I allowed myself to trust another man.

No matter how sexy he was.

"Yeah, I'm not sure I believe that."

I rolled my eyes. "No, you don't want to believe that because the slopes are your life."

"They're not my life." Gray crossed his arms on the bistro table and leaned toward me. His proximity meant it was impossible for me to look anywhere but into his eyes. Eyes that were incredibly warm and sparkled with humor and intelligence. Goddamn this attraction! "They are a big part of it but not my life. I'm not an instructor here. I'm just helping Jacob out—the lodge owner. Grew up in Cunningham Falls so I've been skiing my whole life, know what I'm doing. During high season they can use all the experienced instructors they can find. I own a construction company that takes me around the state but these last few years the winters have been so bad we can't work. Sometimes we get work out of state but not this year, which means my ass is on the slopes. If I'm going to be here anyway I don't mind helping the lodge out when they're struggling to keep up with demand for ski lessons." He smiled. "See, now you know something about me, too."

"Isn't that rough?" I asked, while mentally kicking myself for enjoying conversation with him. "Having months of no work?"

He shrugged. "I've learned to manage it well. The company is successful. I work it so we make enough during the year to see my guys through the winter."

"Your own company. That's impressive for someone your age," I hedged.

Gray chuckled. "You want to know my age, angel, just ask."

"Fine. What age are you?"

"Thirty-three. What age are you?"

"Twenty-five." Thirty-three. Owned his own company. Was definitely confident in his own skin. I suddenly felt too young for him in every way and I was extremely annoyed that this disappointed me. It was, however, also a reality check. It wasn't as if anything could happen between me and Gray. We lived on different continents for a start.

"You're just a baby," he teased.

You have no idea. I decided then and there we had to end this flirtation. I liked him too much. When he smiled I felt that flutter of butterflies. And I had the overwhelming desire to ask him to come to my room for no holds barred sex that would blow my mind, which was so unlike me. Time to put a stop to it all. "I am. Young, I mean, in comparison to you. In more ways than one. Plus, I really, genuinely don't like skiing. Excluding the fact that I broke my leg during a high school skiing trip, I just don't *like* skiing. It's wet and cold." I leaned forward now, too, and ignored the shiver that sprinkled down my spine at the way his eyes dipped automatically to my mouth. "I'm not outdoorsy. At all. I like reading." I gestured with my ereader. "I like shopping. A lot. I like dancing. I like going to the ballet. To the movies. To the theatre. I like cooking. I love baking. I like organizing things, from my well-stocked closet to events. I don't like"—I gestured to him—"skiing, chopping wood, running, mountain biking, hiking, fishing, hunting, or whatever the things are that mountain men like to do." I sat back in my chair, a little breathless with exasperation. "So, I don't know who you think I am but I'm not her."

Gray seemed visibly surprised by my outburst, blinking slowly for a second or two. And then he grinned that wicked, crooked smile of his. "Chopping wood? Hiking? Fishing? Mountain men like me?"

Crap. Had I just been unbearably ignorant? "You don't like all that?"

"I don't chop wood. You can buy it chopped. I hate fishing. It bores the fuck out of me. But I do like hiking, mountain biking, running, and anything else that gets my blood pumping. However"—he leaned toward me—"I don't need *you* to like all those things. Though I have a feeling I can talk you into hiking."

"How's that?"

He studied me carefully. "Saw you come out of the lodge before you came here this morning. You just stopped and stared out across the valley wearing this sweet little smile. You appreciate the beauty of where you are, I can tell. I could take you hiking to some beautiful spots in the summer."

Ah there's the rub. "I won't be here, Gray."

His eyes heated at my soft reply. "I like the way you say my name, angel."

"I'm not an angel."

"You like to bake?"

It was my turn to blink at the random question. "Yes. Do you?"

Gray shook his head. "No, but I sure as shit would love to taste whatever you can bake."

I laughed at his persistence. "You're tireless."

"Yeah. So if you're done trying to put me off—stellar job by the way—will you have dinner with me tonight?"

Before I could answer, a young woman, perhaps a few years younger than me, approached our table wearing snow gear and clutching a to-go cup. "Hey, Gray." She smiled prettily down at him.

He gave her a warm smile in return that immediately made me pay close attention to their interaction. "Whitney, hey."

"You're not going on the slopes today?" She shot me a curious look.

"There doesn't seem to be a need for me today. You booked up?"

"All day." She nodded and looked at me again.

Gray caught it and gestured to me. "Whitney, this is Autumn. Autumn, this is Whitney. Whitney's a ski instructor during high season, college junior otherwise."

She smiled politely at me. "You're a guest?"

"I am." And deciding to try to push Gray again, I blurted, "I take it Gray is the resort's local player? Flirts with all the guests and persistently asks them out to dinner?"

His head snapped my way at the question and I could feel his frown even though I kept my gaze locked on Whitney.

Her eyes widened and she turned back to Gray. "Did you break up with Yvette?"

Yvette? Who was Yvette?

"Almost a year ago," he answered but kept his focus on me.

"I didn't know. I'm sorry." She looked at me. "To answer your question, no, Gray isn't the resort's local player—far from it. Last I heard he was in a serious relationship. But, you know, maybe you should ask him yourself since he's sitting right there." She shot him a look that clearly said 'good luck' and strode out of the coffeehouse.

Squirming a little, I forced myself to meet his gaze.

He did not look happy.

"She has a crush on you," I said for some inane reason.

"I know," he replied through gritted teeth. "I've known her since she was seventeen so it's not going to happen."

I nodded and tried to appear like I didn't care about anything one way or the other.

"Want to tell me what the hell that was about? You got something to ask, babe, you ask me."

I suspected the transition from 'angel' to 'babe' in the endearment department wasn't a good thing, and I hated that it caused this horrible ache in my chest. The truth was just because I couldn't give in to my attraction to Gray didn't mean I wanted him to dislike me.

"I thought I made it clear I'm not trying to play you."

"You did."

"So you want to explain the attitude with Whitney?"

We stared at each other in silence and then he sighed, not hiding his disappointment. "Swear to God, you walked into that restaurant and everything about you drew me like I'd been trekking through snow for days and you were a roaring fucking fire just out of reach. But I guess I was wrong."

Hurt, I flinched, not wanting him to think I was cold.

Frustration crossed his expression. "Now why the hell do I feel like *I* need to apologize?" he practically growled.

"You don't." I shook my head and bravely stared right into his gorgeous eyes while I gave him the truth. "Gray, this can't happen. You want to know why I came here? Because my life is a mess. I have no job, no idea what I want to do with my life, and my last boyfriend hit me and then started to harass me when I broke things off with him for hitting me."

The air at the table suddenly felt stifling as Gray's face darkened with fury.

His intense reaction at once frightened and thrilled me but I forged ahead. "The guy before him stole my money. We decided to open a catering company together, I handed over the start-up funds without any legal paperwork, and he took off with my money instead. There was nothing I could do unless I wanted a long and lengthy legal battle where a court full of people would hear how trusting and foolish I'd been. Before him, my boyfriend cheated with someone I thought was my friend. And before him was my first real boyfriend. He was older than me—looking back, much too old for me—and I learned too late I was one of many 'young things' he liked to 'collect.'" My chest tightened at the anger in Gray's eyes, knowing that it was on my behalf. "I'm not saying I don't trust people, trust men. I've proven time and time again that I wear my heart on my sleeve. And my brother is a prime example that good men exist. But the last guy was kind of the straw that broke the camel's back."

Gray's eyes flared and he gestured to me. "You can't keep all that beauty from some lucky guy because of a couple of assholes."

I smiled at his terse compliment. "I don't intend to. I love being in a relationship too much. I'm an affectionate person. I need that in my life. But the timing is all wrong." I squashed the hope flaring to life in his eyes. "It's not just about what Darren did to me. It's about me. I'm floundering. I came here to try to figure my life out and a guy just can't factor into that."

"Why not? I'm just asking for dinner, angel."

"Exactly. But what if I end up wanting more?" I bit my lip, my heart pounding at putting my honesty out there. Usually I had no problem sharing my true feelings with anyone. But that's how they'd gotten trampled in the past and I had a feeling Gray could really, really hurt me.

His voice turned husky as he leaned even farther across the table. "Angel, I'm hoping you do."

I shook my head, trying to ignore the heat between my thighs at the sexual promise in his gaze. "I mean more than that, too."

I held my breath, waiting for him to flee.

Instead he studied my face with a sweet reverence that made me want to meet him across that table with my mouth. "Fuck me," he muttered, "you're right. Heart on your sleeve."

He finally understood, which made me blush like an idiot.

That for some reason made his expression soften to a look of such tenderness I felt a little breathless. "You gotta know I think you're the sweetest fucking woman I've ever met."

I huffed, blushing harder. My goodness, I'd never blushed so much in my life. "You don't know me."

"I think I'm starting to. And what I do know, I really like." Sudden determination hardened his features. "Have dinner with me tonight."

Startled laughter burst out of me before I could stop it. "Didn't you hear anything I said?"

"Yeah, I did. Every word. And I'm going to prove to you that there are men ready to treat you like the angel you are and I'm one of them."

"It's just physical attraction, Gray." Even I heard the panic in my voice.

It made him reach out and thread his callused fingers through mine and I couldn't stop the flutters in my belly. "After what you just laid out, do you really think I'd keep on you if all I wanted to do was fuck you and walk away?"

I flushed hot at the thought. "Gray."

"Though"—his voice lowered—"you laid it out so I'm laying it out.

I do want you in my bed."

My breathing stuttered at the sudden flurry of images his words provoked. "Gray."

"Keep saying my name in that breathy voice, in that sexy accent, angel, and I'm going to haul you out of here and up to the condo I've rented across the way."

My fingers tightened in his, unwittingly letting him know I wanted that, and Gray groaned. "You're killing me."

I wrenched my hand out of his and sat back. "We can't."

He shook his head. "Not leaving here until you agree to dinner."

My God, I'd thought Killian was the most stubborn man I'd ever known but Grayson King could give him a run for his money. I let out a shaky breath. "Fine. Dinner tonight. But on one condition."

Triumph and something I thought might be anticipation smoldered in his gaze. "Anything."

"If I decide that whatever this is between us ends at dinner tonight, you'll respect that decision and leave me alone."

He didn't hide that he hated the idea but he held out his hand and offered, "Deal."

I tentatively accepted his handshake, concerned by how delicious even that simple touch felt. Just as I went to release his hold, his tightened and he pulled me across the table. I let out a surprised gasp as he leaned in to whisper in my ear, "Just warning you: I'm going to make sure you want another date."

Goosebumps cascaded down my neck at the feel of his warm breath on my ear and I felt my nipples tighten.

Oh God.

Then he released me and I slumped back in my seat, staring up at him, I'm sure dazedly, as he towered over me with a promise in his blue gaze. "What's your room number?"

I gave him it without thinking it through.

"That one of the suites?"

"Yes."

His brow wrinkled. "Look forward to hearing how you can swing that on no job, angel."

"I—"

"Tonight." He cut me off. "You can tell me tonight. I'll pick you up at seven."

"Okay."

He gave me one last assessing look before he turned and walked out of the café.

Feeling completely thrown, confused, excited, scared, and more confused, I looked down at my ereader and wondered what Killian would say if he found out I had feelings for a man I'd just met. He would not be happy. I knew that. Shit.

Before I could let that thought fester, something made me look up and I watched with widening eyes as Gray marched back through the snow toward the coffeehouse. His features were taut with tension and I wondered what the heck had happened in less than a minute to put that expression on his face.

I would understand seconds later when he threw open the coffeehouse door, strode purposefully toward me, and my now pounding heart, curled a hand around my wrist, and hauled me out of my seat with such force I collided against him.

His arm banded tight around my waist while his other hand tangled through my hair to clasp the back of my head. It all happened so fast I had no time to stop the crush of his lips against mine.

I gasped into his mouth in surprise and he took the opening, his tongue tangling with mine.

And that was how I received the deepest, wettest, sexiest kiss of my life.

I clung to him as fire lashed across my skin. I wanted to burrow into him, feel every inch of Grayson King wrapped around me. Thankfully *he* remembered we were in public and reluctantly broke the kiss but not his hold on me.

Staring up into his eyes in a lust-filled fog, slowly the titters from the other customers in the café filtered into my awareness and I tensed against Gray.

He felt it and his grip on me tightened. Then he treated me to a shivery brush of his gorgeous mouth against mine and he said, his voice hoarse, "Best. Fucking. Kiss. Ever."

At that I laughed because as crazy as it was, it was also bloody true. "Ever," I agreed as he grinned back at me.

Then, like he couldn't help himself, he brushed his mouth over mine once more, gave me a squeeze, and said, "Tonight."

Then he abruptly let me go.

I was still standing, watching him walk out of the coffeehouse and across the snow toward the condos when it occurred to me that as much as I loved my brother, I suddenly couldn't care less if Killian was happy or not that I had feelings for a man I'd just met.

Grayson King was unlike any man I'd ever been kissed by before and I knew even if I fought it, I'd only end up kissing him again. Deep down, in my secret heart of hearts, I knew I wanted him more than I wanted to be sensible.

Chapter Four

A knock sounded on my door at seven o' clock and I blew out a shaky breath.

When I told Catie and Kyle I was going on a date with Gray, Kyle had looked pensive while Catie beamed from ear to ear.

"You came here to relax, Autumn. I can't think of a better way to do that than multiple orgasms via Hot Mountain Man."

Kyle had wandered off at that point, not wishing to participate in that kind of conversation.

"Multiple orgasms, really?" I'd laughed. "You know that how?"

"Because he gave you the best kiss ever—your words—and I refuse to believe a man that looks like Grayson King isn't capable of giving a woman fantastic orgasms. I couldn't live in a world where that wasn't true."

Suffice it to say Catie was all for me having a fling on my ski retreat. Therefore I couldn't bring myself to tell her I knew deep in my gut that this thing between me and Gray was so far beyond fling material it wasn't even funny. However, I didn't want my best friend to think I was crazy or naïve, so I didn't confide that to her.

Moreover, when Killian and Skylar called earlier I'd left all mention of Gray out. My brother would stew with worry if he knew I'd met a man over here.

As I'd gotten ready for dinner, those butterflies came back. To be fair, I'd had them all day but as the time for our date approached they began fluttering around in my belly like wild things. Assuming we'd be dining at the only nice restaurant on the resort, I put on a pair of black cigarette trousers with a silk long-sleeved shirt tucked into them. The shirt was my signature color—emerald green. I'd left a few buttons undone, showing a sexy hint of cleavage. Years ago Killian had bought me a rose gold necklace with a delicate chain and an even more delicate diamond 'A' pendant. The A nestled seductively between my breasts, catching the light every time I moved, drawing attention. Like always, my hair was down, and I wore a pair of sexy as hell sky high Jimmy Choos. They were rose gold lamé with criss-cross straps. A delicate rose gold bracelet and matching ring, along with an emerald green clutch, finished the look.

It was fair to say I'd brought way too many clothes with me on this trip but now that I'd met Gray, I was glad for the choices.

My outfit was sexy but to me wearing trousers sent a message—I wasn't looking to get laid tonight. This was just dinner.

When I opened my hotel door Gray's expression suggested that message had not been received. He put a big hand on my waist and leaned in, and I braced for a kiss like the one at the coffeehouse. Instead he surprised me with a lip brush across my cheekbone and then he released me, stepping back out of my personal space.

"You look beautiful."

I stared at him, tingling from head to toe from his gentlemanly kiss. "Thank you. You look great, too."

And he did. He wore a dark green shirt with his suit trousers and I wondered if he'd subconsciously chosen green because I wore it a lot.

He held out a hand. "Shall we?"

I hesitated, knowing as soon as I took his hand, I wouldn't want to let go.

Sensing my uncertainty, Gray reassured me, "Just dinner, Autumn."

That was when I discovered something more dangerous than Gray's ability to give me butterflies. He also made me feel safe.

Taking his hand, trying not to shiver at the way the rough skin of his palm felt against mine, I let go of the breath I was holding. I tried to relax as we strolled hand-in-hand toward the restaurant.

"If it was up to me I'd take you to dinner in town but I thought you'd feel more relaxed if we stayed somewhere familiar tonight."

"I do, thank you."

He smiled and then his gaze dropped to my shoes before returning to my face. He grinned. "Never dated a woman on my eye level before."

"Well, I'm wearing five-inch heels."

"I noticed. They're sexy as fuck."

Our eyes held for what felt like forever and he squeezed my hand. I blinked and jerked my gaze away, trying to catch my breath.

"So what height does that make you out of heels?" he suddenly asked.

"Five nine. What height are you?"

"Six three."

"Tall," I muttered, trying not to imagine that long, hard body of his covering me in bed …and epically failing.

His warm hand tightened in mine as if he could read my expression. "I promised myself I'd be a gentleman tonight and that's going to be hard to do when you've got me thinking about how long your legs are and how amazing they'll feel wrapped around me… so maybe we should stop talking about this."

I had to curb nervous laughter because I had a feeling it wasn't going to take much to lead either of our thoughts into the bedroom. "Sounds like a plan," I choked out.

We reached the restaurant in no time (thank goodness) and the hostess, who was as familiar with Gray as everyone else at the lodge appeared to be, led us directly to a table by the massive picture window at the back of the room. The sun had already set but from our table we could see part of the valley where the town was lit up in the dark. It was beautiful.

We ordered our drinks and I dragged my gaze from the view to Gray to find him studying me thoughtfully.

I pressed a hand to my cheek. "Do I have something on my face?"

He shook his head. "No. It's just hard to want to look anywhere but at you."

The compliment caused a small bark of incredulous laughter. "I don't know whether you're feeding me lines or if you're being genuine. Unbelievably, I think you're being genuine."

Gray scowled. "I already told you I'm not feeding you a line and I thought after our kiss today you understood where we're at."

"Our kiss?"

His eyes narrowed. "You can't deny the chemistry between us, angel."

"I'm not trying to." I sighed and it sounded shaky. "I'm sorry.

I'm… I'm not used to men complimenting me just because they want to and not because they're hoping it will lead somewhere."

Understanding crossed his expression. "Yeah, I'll bet."

Needing the conversation to turn to something I could deal with, I gestured toward the town. "So you grew up in Cunningham Falls?"

"Yeah. My family has lived there for generations."

"Big family?"

"Pretty big. Immediate family it's only my parents and my brother Noah. But we have cousins and aunts and uncles who have lived here for generations, too, so it's never really felt like just the four of us."

"Is Noah in construction?"

Gray grinned like I'd said something funny. "Not even close. My brother owns Spread Your Wings Sanctuary. A wild bird sanctuary. He's like the bird whisperer."

"Wow, that's cool." And it was. I'd never owned a pet because my uncle wouldn't allow us to have one but I loved animals and immediately liked anyone who had an affinity with them. I'd often contemplated getting a dog but I wasn't home a lot and I didn't think it would be fair to leave a pet on his/her own for so long every day. "Are you two very different then?"

"Yes and no." He shrugged. "Different personalities but same values. Hard not to grow up with the same values in the extended King family. We're all close. Got a good family. I'm lucky."

Gray *was* lucky. I couldn't imagine what it was like to grow up in such a big, loving family. I know I was lucky to have Killian, but it would have been nice for us both to have that kind of support outside of each other. The wistfulness I felt must have shown in my eyes because Gray's filled with questions. Guessing what they were likely to be and not ready to answer them, I continued to guide the conversation. "And Yvette?" I said, referring to the woman Whitney had mentioned earlier in the day.

He leaned forward, bracing his crossed arms on the table, his expression casual. I searched for pain or anger in his eyes but saw nothing but calm. "My ex-fiancée."

Whoa. Okay. *Fiancée.* Why did that cause a painful twist in my chest?

"We broke up nearly a year ago. We'd been together five years. She proposed to me." He rubbed the back of his neck, suddenly looking uncomfortable. "I didn't like it. I know that probably makes me a macho man dick in your eyes but I didn't want to be proposed to. It was up to me to do the proposing."

I shrugged, not bothered by this in the least, because frankly, as a romantic, I'd want to be proposed to. "You're a traditionalist."

"Yeah, when it comes to that shit I am. I said yes because I loved her and I didn't want to hurt her. But over the years I managed to somehow put her off anytime she broached the subject of wedding planning. Finally everything came to a head. She pushed for me to set a date and I finally realized I loved her but the connection wasn't there. We broke it off. *I* broke it off."

Oh wow. I suddenly felt sorry for Yvette.

"I felt like shit about it, for not knowing my own mind, but looking back I know there was a part of me deep down that knew she wasn't the one. I just couldn't admit that to myself, or her, for a really long time."

I tilted my head in contemplation because I was surprised by the information he'd just imparted. "You believe in 'the one'?"

Gray swallowed, almost as if he was nervous. "I do now."

The air around us grew still at what he'd just implied.

Holy …

"Gray," I whispered, not knowing what to say.

I found I loved what he was implying but it scared the absolute bejesus out of me, too.

"Never felt about her the way I feel about you and I've only just met you," he continued, holding my gaze in his.

"Are you ready to order?" The waiter suddenly appeared, giving me a chance to collect my thoughts.

Once he had our order, I turned back to my dinner date. "We should think about this before it goes any further."

He shook his head. "We can do that later."

Panic made the butterflies in my belly flutter up toward my heart, their wings kicking it into hyper speed. "No, we can't because I live on the other side of a pretty big ocean and that's not a small problem. We should discuss what that means before we go any further."

"No."

"No?"

"No. I want it so our hooks are so deep in each other it doesn't matter what problems we face, we'll do whatever we can to overcome them together."

"This is insane. We just met!"

"Yeah, we did. And yeah, it's crazy." He leaned across the table again, his voice pitched low and sexy. "But tell me you don't feel like you've known me forever. Tell me it's not just about sex. You feel it, I know you do. This is more than just amazing sexual attraction. There's a connection here, angel."

"How can that be? How do you know?"

"I don't know how I know. I just do. If people knew how this shit worked, someone would have written a formula for it by now so everybody got a piece of the good life."

"Oh my God." My fingers trembled as I reached up to push my hair off my face.

"We stumbled onto something special, Autumn. We would be fools to turn our backs on it when other folks aren't so lucky."

"You don't know anything about me." I continued to deny him.

"Then tell me. I told you about my family. Tell me about yours."

The fact was, after hearing about his big family, I wasn't so sure about telling him about mine. Although part of me was looking for an excuse to break the inexplicable bond between us, the other part of me was afraid that if I told him about my upbringing he might decide we *were* too different.

And how messed-up was that?

He'd turned my emotions into a war unto themselves.

"Autumn?"

I glanced out of the window toward the town he'd grown up in. "I'm from Glasgow. I have a big brother, Killian. He's my half-brother, really—we had different dads—but that's just a technicality. He's my brother."

"*Had?*" Gray picked up on the past tense immediately.

I looked back at him, and found his gaze curious. There was a small crease line between his brows that hinted at concern. "His dad is still alive but he wasn't his dad. He's Killian's father and there's a difference. He's been in and out of prison most of Killian's life. Mum met *my* dad when Killian was little and my dad adopted him, so he was really *our* dad. But they uh… when I was six and Killian was eleven we were on holiday with Mum and Dad and… our parents died in a helicopter accident."

Suddenly Gray reached across the table and threaded his fingers through mine. "Shit, I'm sorry."

I melted at the warmth in his expression. It was mixed with a sympathetic pain and I knew, deep down, that his emotion for me was genuine. It boggled my mind but it was true. Gray hurt when I hurt. How strange but beautiful was that?

"I'm okay. It was a long time ago. But it meant that Killian and I were raised by his biological father's brother and James Byrne is not the nicest of men. He sued the events company, and their insurance company, and he won a lot of money for us. He's very smart and has the golden touch when it comes to finances. He took that money and invested it for us in some high risk ventures that *paid off*. We each got our share when we turned eighteen. A lot of mine is still in investment and stock funds and it means I can live well. Hence the suite. But I'll have to find a job sooner or later. It's not the kind of money that will last a lifetime. And I want a job.

"My uncle didn't think it was necessary for me to have one. He's delusional enough to think that me not having a job proved to the rest of the world that he was wealthy enough for his niece to live like a socialite. When I was younger he 'indulged me'—his words, not mine— and paid for me to continue my ballet lessons in the hope that any future success as a ballerina would give him social standing. But when I was thirteen I auditioned for the Royal Conservatoire of Scotland, which is one of the world's top five schools of performing arts and extremely competitive. I didn't get in. My uncle refused to pay for any further ballet lessons if he couldn't parade me out to all his friends as if my ballet achievements were owed all to him."

"And is that all he cared about?" Gray squeezed my hand. "Money and what you could do for his reputation?"

I nodded. "Our uncle gave us nothing but material offerings. No affection. No family. Killian stepped in and became my parent and he was just a child himself. He loved and protected me with a fierceness that meant I had what I needed growing up. It wasn't a mum and dad but he tried his damn best. I guess because I had Killian, my uncle's lack of affection didn't hurt as much. But Killian didn't have that same paternal support and so he grew up trying to win it from our uncle. He even took a job at my uncle's record label. I hated watching him trying to prove himself to a man who didn't deserve the attempt."

"Your brother still work for him?"

I shook my head and smiled. "He met someone. You may have heard of her actually. Skylar Finch?"

He frowned. "The name is familiar but I don't know why."

"She's been all over the news lately. She used to be the frontwoman for the band Tellurian. Her parents were murdered. She fell off the face of the earth a few years ago and just showed up again recently."

Gray nodded as recognition lit his eyes. "I do remember catching glimpses of that in the news."

"Well, she was living in Glasgow. It's a long story." I shrugged. "But the result was that Killian fell in love with her. She's changed him for the better. Now he's starting up his own record company and our uncle is out of our lives for good. We don't need his toxic personality around us anyway."

In answer, Gray rubbed his thumb over the top of my hand and I fought a shiver. "First your uncle and then all those assholes you told me about. Fuck, Autumn, you deserve so much more than that."

"What if that's not true?" I whispered because the words were hard to say. "What if I'm not who you want me to be and this is just a giant mistake?"

"I get it. I get why you're questioning this because it feels unreal that two people could connect like this so quickly. You ever ask why I'm not questioning it? It's because I know that this kind of connection exists and it's real. I know that because I was lucky enough to grow up surrounded by love. I'm more open to it. I get it now why you're not. Between those guys and everything you've lost, I get it in a way that I really wish I didn't. Because I've known you only a few days and I would give anything to give you back your parents. That's why you don't want to believe this is true. Because good things rarely happen, right?"

"That makes me sound ungrateful. I've lived a privileged life."

"No. You have money. There's a difference and you know it. You know it better than anyone."

I gripped his hand tight, feeling tears burn my eyes. "I'd give it back in a heartbeat."

"I know, angel," he murmured, taking hold of my other hand.

Suddenly my chest felt constricted as a wave of feelings toward him crashed into me. "I'm scared."

"Don't be. I promise you there's nothing to be scared of from me. This is the real fucking deal and I'm going to protect it with everything I have. Just say you're with me."

"I live in Glasgow," I reiterated, hanging on by a thread.

"Forget that. Forget everything but you and me and right now. I don't care if that's reckless or stupid… I just… Just give yourself over to this with me and I honestly believe it will all work itself out. Will you do that? Will you just hold on with me?"

I stared into his face, a face that felt so strangely familiar to me now. My fears rode me but I knew as the warmth and excitement and thrill and peace exploded through me in opposing harmony that he was going to win over my fears.

I nodded, my hands tightening in his. "I'll hold on."

Chapter Five

The rest of our dinner conversation was balanced between heavy and light. I told him about Skylar being homeless in Glasgow, about helping her start a homeless shelter charity now that she was healthy and happy again. I spoke more about Killian and how overprotective he was (which didn't even faze Gray). Gray talked about his parents and brother, and his cousins Josh and Zach and their families. We learned about each other's food, music, movie likes and dislikes, and he made me laugh. A lot.

We moved to the bar after our meal and time flew. I was disappointed when I realized we had to say goodnight. However, Gray kept his word. In fact, he didn't even kiss me goodnight. Well, not a real kiss… but what he did was almost better.

Somehow he managed to give me the most spine-tingling kiss goodnight with a mere brush of his mouth against the corner of mine. Seriously, I almost melted into a puddle at his feet as his head pulled back from the kiss. He caressed my cheekbone with the pad of his thumb and then stepped back, wishing me goodnight.

With the promise of seeing him tomorrow in the air, I'd fled into my suite before I did something I'd regret—like throw myself at him when he was trying so hard to be a gentleman.

He was booked for morning ski lessons, something I knew he now regretted, but he'd promised Jacob he'd help him out and it would seem

Gray didn't back out of a promise. I liked that. I liked that a lot.

To be fair, I liked everything about him.

"Oh my God, you are so cute," Catie teased at breakfast the next morning.

I made a face at both her and her grinning husband. "I am not."

"You are, too. You're sitting there gazing dreamily out at the snowy mountains wondering if your Prince Charming is one of those moving dots in the powder."

I rolled my eyes to hide the fact that she was right. "Am not."

"Are too. We can safely assume the date went well?"

I glanced between Catie and Kyle, wondering if I told them the truth if they'd think I was crazy.

Catie frowned, sensing my concern. "What is it?"

I lowered my cup of tea. "You'll both think I'm insane."

"Why? What is it?"

I exhaled slowly. "I think he… okay, I know this sounds nuts and I would think it was nuts if it wasn't happening to me but… I think he might be… well… *the one*." I flinched, bracing for their reaction.

When all I got was silence, I slumped in my seat. "You think I'm nuts."

"I don't." Kyle shrugged. "I knew Catie was it for me the moment we met."

I smiled as Catie stared adoringly at her husband. "You did?"

"Aye." He grinned back at her. "I felt like you'd slammed into me the moment I saw you because I couldn't catch my breath. And I knew. I just knew you were it."

"You've never told me that before." She smacked his shoulder.

He winced while I laughed. "Well, I didn't want to sound like a total Muppet. But Autumn's being honest and I don't want her to feel like an idiot. This shite can happen." He turned to me. "But beware. Next thing you know you're married at twenty-two."

I chuckled. "I'm twenty-five."

"You know what I mean. Catie and I met at twenty-one and less than a year later we got married."

"I knew I loved him right away, too," Catie said to me before turning back to Kyle, "but I didn't know you felt the same way. You didn't even say that in your vows!"

"I think getting engaged after six months and then getting married five months later pretty much says it all, babe."

She snorted. "True."

Not wanting to interrupt the warm moment between them but needing reassurance, I asked, "So you don't think I'm nuts?"

"No," they said in unison.

Catie continued, "However, men haven't always treated you the way you deserve. One of them not too long ago. Be careful."

I stiffened at the reminder I hadn't been very good at choosing men. "I know that. But have I ever said any of them were *the one*? Gray... Gray would never hurt me. I don't know how I know that. I just do."

My friends contemplated me in silence for a while again until I was squirming with the need to bolt out of my seat. Then Catie reached across the table for my hand, like Gray had done last night, and squeezed it in hers. "You want to know what I think?"

No, I'm scared. "Yes?"

"I think after everything you've been through, the fact that you still have the biggest, most open heart of anyone I know, makes you the bravest person I know. Christ, Autumn, it is so much easier to hide from love than it is to give in to it. You're such a special person and if you think this guy is the one then go for it. We'll be here no matter what happens."

Tears glistened in my eyes. "You're the best friend ever."

She grinned. "I know."

I laughed but my amusement faded when I whispered, "Killian won't be so understanding."

"This isn't his life. Who knows whether this connection with Gray will go anywhere... but you'll never know if you don't take a shot at it. However, if you need me to say it, I'll say it: *I* trust you, Autumn. Trust yourself."

Before I could stop them, the tears spilled over. "Best. Friend. Ever."

* * * *

Now that Catie and Kyle emotionally had my back, I felt even more antsy to see Gray so we could further explore the immense connection between us. Which meant, without any spa appointments booked that day, I was bored and impatient as I lounged around the lodge. Eventually I found myself snuggled up in the corner of one of the couches in the reception area, my back to the fire, my knees drawn up with a notepad on them. My boots lay scattered beside me on the floor and there was a glass of warm cider on the window ledge by the couch.

I stared at the piece of paper I'd torn free from the notepad braced on my knee, chewing the end of my pen in thought.

POSSIBLE CAREER OPTIONS

1. Small catering company (on my own this time!!)
2. Bakery? Or catering company focused on baked goods only
3. Stylist to the stars (not realistic but I did a good job with Skylar)
4. Event organizer/wedding planner
5. PA at Killian's new label--job is ready and waiting
6. Interior designer. No experience! Would be fun though!
7. AHHHH!
8. I suck
9. HOLD ME :(

I felt the heat of him at my back before he said, "What are you doing?"

I tilted my head back to find Gray leaning over me, looking down at my notebook. He was upside down to me but I could still see his eyes scanning the paper. I clamped a hand over it. "Nothing."

Gray rounded the couch. He was dressed in dark jeans, winter boots, a navy knit sweater with a roll neck, and a winter jacket. His face was flushed from the cold and he vibrated with an air of masculine energy that created a shot of tingles between my legs. He smiled at me before leaning down to brush his lips against my cheek. My eyes fluttered closed at the sensation, which was why it was so easy for him to slide the bit of paper out from under my hand.

"Hey!" I cried belatedly, throwing my legs off the couch to stand up and reach for it.

But I was in socks and now significantly shorter than I had been the night before so he held the list high above him and out of reach.

"Give me," I huffed, jumping for it.

Gray laughed and wrapped his arm around my waist, pulling me against him so suddenly that I was immediately distracted by the feel of his hard chest beneath my hands.

He looked down into my face and his arm tightened around me. "You feel good here, angel."

I frowned because I felt *amazing* against him but he still had my bit of paper. "Give me my notes."

Instead he kissed me. Properly. Tongue and all. It was such a deep, luscious, hungry kiss, I curled my fingers into his sweater just to hold on. I swear my legs were trembling when he finally let me up for air. Gray released me with another soft caress of his lips and then snuggled me into his side as he brought the paper down to his eye level.

He was already reading it before I fully recovered from his kiss.

"Okay," he said after a few seconds perusal. "Our plans for today just changed."

"Our plans? What were our plans?"

"Honestly?"

I nodded, lost in his gaze.

He grinned, seemingly totally aware of how much he affected me. "Me fighting hard not to drag you to the nearest bedroom like a caveman."

I gave a huff of laughter. "I'm sure."

"But now I need to put those thoughts on hold." He squeezed me again. "I think I've got a way to test your options." He waved the bit of paper in the air. "Five birds, one stone. If you're up for doing that while you're here? Say you got the opportunity to cater, organize an event, style someone, and redecorate a room this week? See which one you enjoyed or succeeded at most?"

Bemused, I nodded. "I would do it. I don't know how I can possibly do it here though."

"Boots and jacket on. I'll show you."

As soon as I did as asked, Gray took over pulling my hat down over my hair as I tugged on gloves. He pressed a sweet kiss to the tip of my nose before he let me go. "Come on." He slid his arm along my shoulder and pulled me into his side, so I put my arm around his waist to make it easier for us as we walked. It was amazing how natural it felt to be in his arms as he led us across the car park toward the building that housed the holiday apartments.

As we approached the outer staircase of the building I remembered

Gray said he was staying in one of the condos. "I thought you said you *weren't* going to drag me to the nearest bed?"

He chuckled. "I'm not."

"Oh." It came out sounding way more disappointed than I meant it to and Gray threw his head back in deep, rumbling, attractive laughter. I found myself staring at him as he did so, loving that I made him laugh like that.

"Soon," he promised. "But today I want you to meet someone. Some*ones* actually. Molly and Susan Olsen. They're here on a girl trip. They lost Molly's younger brother to cancer nine months ago and reading between the lines, things have been hard with Susan's husband ever since. He's not here with them. Susan decided to bring Molly here for her thirteenth birthday because Molly has always wanted to learn to ski and they don't live far from Cunningham Falls. I gave them both lessons a couple of days ago and then again this morning and Molly was going on and on about missing out on a birthday party."

We trudged upstairs to the first floor. "That's so sad about her brother."

"Yeah, it is, angel." Gray led me to a door near the very end of the walkway. "But I'm hoping we can make at least today a little better for them."

Behind the door I could hear the murmur of conversation and when Gray knocked on it, it flew open almost immediately.

"Gray, did we forget something?" an attractive blonde with light green eyes asked. She was dressed in snow trousers but wearing only a T-shirt.

"Gray!" A cute miniature version of the woman pushed into her mother's side. She was still dressed in a pink snowsuit. "You're back." Her eyes drifted to me and I saw them widen with curiosity.

"Susan, Molly, I want you to meet my woman, Autumn. Autumn, this is Susan and Molly."

I smiled and shook their hands, reeling from having just been referred to as Gray's "woman." It was so macho mountain man and the feminist in me should have been affronted. The possessive, hungry woman in me, however, won out and wanted to enforce this claim by getting extremely naked with him.

"I know Molly said she was sad not to get a birthday party so I brought Autumn to help out." He nudged me forward and stood behind me, his hands resting on my shoulders. "You have in Autumn, Wonder Woman. She can cook, bake, event organize, interior design slash decorate and is literally a stylist to the stars—she styled Skylar Finch."

Molly's eyes grew huge at this information while what Gray was doing suddenly sunk in. "You know Skylar Finch?"

Since it was all over the news anyway and Molly had a "fangirl" light in her eyes I nodded. "She's dating my brother."

"You're Killian O'Dea's sister!" she practically shrieked, jumping a little. Susan let out a little burst of surprised laughter at her daughter's reaction.

Gray dipped his head toward mine and I glanced back and up at him to find him grinning at me. "Think she knows who Skylar Finch is, angel."

I shook with laughter and turned back to Molly. "I am Killian's sister."

"That. Is. So. Cool."

"So... does that mean you'd be good with Autumn organizing your birthday party, handling catering, decoration, and helping you and your mom find an outfit?"

"Oh my God, yes! Mom, please?" She turned to Susan.

Susan cupped her daughter's cheek and stared at her in a way that made me feel like she was sad and happy at the same time. "Of course, honey."

"You good with that?" Gray asked me.

My smile couldn't have been bigger. Give a little girl and her mother something good after something so awful had happened to them. Yeah, I was good with that. "I am so in."

His expression softened to such tenderness I melted into him. "Knew you would be." He turned his gaze to Susan. "How about I drive you girls into town, you get the supplies you need, we'll do lunch, and I'll bring you back up the mountain?"

"Are you an angel?" Susan said, shaking her head in amazement.

Gray squeezed my shoulders. "Nah, just found myself one."

I rolled my eyes at his cheesiness as Susan laughed...but inwardly my knees turned to jelly.

"Okay, Mols, go back into the apartment and get changed out of the snow suit."

"Yay!" Molly did a funny little victory dance. "I'm going to text

Addy right now and tell her I just met Skylar Finch's boyfriend's sister!" She disappeared into the apartment.

Susan's eyes were bright when she looked back at us. "I haven't seen her this engaged or excited since..." Grief darkened her expression. "Well... thank you."

"Happy to help," I said, my words low and soft because they were constricted by emotion. I didn't even know this woman but the pain radiating from her was palpable. I just wanted to wrap my arms around her and hold her tight.

She blinked back tears and clapped her hands together. "Let's talk budget before Molly gets back. Do you think you can do everything on five hundred dollars—including outfits?"

"I can definitely do that."

Susan let me into the condo so I could get a sense of the space for decorating. The apartment was open-plan and airy, with a wonderful picture window in the kitchen that looked out over the snow-covered evergreens. There wasn't a lot I could do to it interior-wise, other than decorate, but I already had thoughts stewing.

Twenty minutes later, after I hurried back to the lodge to grab my purse (even though Gray told me I wouldn't need it) and to get my phone so I could text Catie to let her know where I'd be, I walked out into the car park and found Gray standing by a black Chevrolet Tahoe.

"Nice." I patted the side of his SUV as I approached him.

He immediately wrapped an arm around me to draw me against him while we waited for Molly and Susan, and I realized that he hadn't stopped touching me all morning. It was like he couldn't help himself and I loved it. I was a very affectionate person and I liked to be touched and cuddled—probably because I didn't get a lot of that growing up— and the way I felt when Gray touched me was akin to that of an addict grateful for her latest fix.

"Thanks. Best SUV for the snow," he explained.

I nodded but thoughts of his four-by-four were long gone as soon as he pulled me into his embrace. I tipped my head back to look directly into his gorgeous eyes. "How did you know I'd be cool with doing this for Molly and Susan?"

"Everything you told me about what you did for Skylar. And just... you. You're kind, Autumn. It's just who you are. You have the kindest eyes I've ever seen."

I blushed at the compliment, lowering my gaze. "I'm just doing what anyone would do. Molly and Susan have been through something unimaginable. Anyone would want to help make their day a little brighter."

"Not just anyone." He gently raised my chin so I'd meet his eyes. "Susan's a good woman, putting her kid before her grief, trying to give her something, remind her that they're alive and they need to live. Reading between the lines, her husband hasn't been able to do that and not having that kind of support after losing a kid... Well, I can't imagine. And Molly's a cute kid. Always saying please, thank you—appreciative, you know. But now she's a kid who knows something she shouldn't know already—that the people you love can be gone in an instant. It sucks she learned that lesson so young and that's something you know about more than anyone."

Tears pricked my eyes.

"I wanted to do something for them but what could *I* do? But you... you can do something for them. And I can drive you safely down and back up the mountain."

My hands were resting on his chest and as overwhelming emotion flooded me I slid them up to wrap them around his neck. I drew up onto my tiptoes and pressed the softest, sweetest kiss to his lips. When I pulled back I whispered, "Tonight you're mine, Grayson King."

His grip on me turned almost bruising as his eyes darkened. His voice was hoarse when he replied, "I cannot fucking wait, angel."

I grinned and lowered down to the soles of my feet. Gray looked like he wanted to say something more but suddenly Susan and Molly appeared, Molly practically vibrating with excitement.

Chapter Six

I was immediately enamored with Cunningham Falls. It was everything I imagined small town Montana to be—charming, friendly, beautifully snow-covered, and a world away from the city of Glasgow.

After driving expertly down the mountain, Gray stopped first at a coffee shop called Drips & Sips so I was fully caffeinated before we began our shopping adventure. Then Gray left us to it. He gave me and Susan his cell number and told us to call when we were ready to go to lunch. Gray was considerate, thoughtful, and sweet, but he was also a man in the traditional sense and shopping was something he just did not do.

Susan, Molly, and I chattered easily as we wandered around the small town together. Nothing could (or ever would) erase the hard glint of grief in either of their eyes, but Molly was excited and Susan seemed to be relieved by this renewed energy in her daughter. I talked to Molly about the ideas I had for décor and she loved them. I'd been worried it was a little too old for a thirteen-year-old's birthday party but it would seem Molly was over "little girl stuff" and wanted something more sophisticated.

We stopped by Brooke's Blooms, a flower shop, and although the budget didn't allow for too many floral arrangements, we ordered a few in pinks and whites to be delivered to the condo on their last day of vacation, the day we were hosting the party.

It didn't take long for us to realize that as beautiful as Cunningham Falls was, I wasn't going to be able to do everything I needed to do from here. I picked up a bunch of fairy lights for the decoration, and I advised Susan and Molly on really cute outfits we bought from a store called Dress It Up, but we were soon to be stumped on the rest of the planning.

Deciding to have a late lunch, we held off on calling Gray and went back to the coffee shop with its free wifi. We sat at a table with my phone in hand and together we ordered everything online. Moreover, we sent e-invites to all of Molly's friends and a couple of Susan's and some family members.

Finally we called Gray and he took us to a place called Ed's Diner for lunch where I had the best burger I'd had in a long time. Molly threw question after question at Gray, gazing up at him like he was a hero come to life. I sensed an adorable crush.

I couldn't blame her.

At lunch, as soon as Molly took a breath and I had an in, I asked Gray where I could get all my baking and cooking needs. That was the store we hit last and Gray said I could use the condo in his kitchen to cater the party.

It was a fun day but obviously a lot more energetic than Molly or Susan had experienced in a while. Between the ski lessons that morning and walking all over the small town that afternoon, they were tired. We bundled all of my supplies into the car and headed back up the mountain.

I told them I'd see them the next day and received a hug from Molly, followed by a tight squeeze of a hug from her mum. My eyes brightened with tears at the quiet desperation in her grip and I held her just as tight. When we finally let go of each other she smiled gratefully and then touched Gray's arm in silent thanks. He gave her a solemn chin nod and we watched as mother and daughter climbed the stairs up to their condo.

Finally Gray turned to me. "Good day then?"

I nodded, knowing I couldn't hide what I felt for him.

His eyes darkened with desire and a whole lot more. "Tired?"

I shook my head.

Gray's lips curled at the corners. "You ever going to talk again?"

"I'm afraid of what I might say."

He stepped into me, sliding his arms around my waist to pull me close. "Don't be. Ever. Not with me."

Melting against him, I slid my hands across his chest, desperate to feel every inch of him against me. "Will you do a late dinner with me tonight?"

"You don't even have to ask."

"And then after… do you want to spend the night with me?"

I felt his heart beat faster against the palm of my hand. "More than I want anything."

* * * *

I didn't remember much about dinner that evening. I did remember the look on Gray's face when I met him outside the restaurant (something I insisted on because I knew if he collected me from my suite we wouldn't make it to dinner). I wore an LBD—a little black dress. It was simple but form fitting, and although the sweetheart neckline only hinted at cleavage, and the hem sat a respectable few inches above the knee, it was still sexy. Especially paired with my Jimmy Choos. And by the smoldering heat in Gray's eyes, he thought so too.

I remembered how gorgeous he looked in a cobalt blue shirt that matched his eyes.

I remembered that I hardly ate a thing because I was so nervous and excited about what was going to happen between us *after* dinner.

But I couldn't remember our conversation. All I was cognizant of was the palpable heat between us. Both of our minds were on one thing and one thing only.

Suffice it to say we rushed dinner.

In fact, in retrospect it was almost comical how fast we hurried down the corridor to my suite, hand in hand. However, neither of us were laughing. At the time, there wasn't anything funny about the potent sexual desire licking between us like flames scorching our skin.

My hands trembled as I fumbled in my clutch for my room key card and as soon as that door opened, Gray pushed me gently inside, let the door slam shut, and then shoved me against the wall, pinning me there with his body and his mouth as he crushed mine beneath his.

I wrapped myself around him, wanting us to melt together, and my fingers curled in the hair at the back of his neck as I licked and sucked and flicked my tongue against his, our kiss so deep I'd forgotten where we were. All that mattered was Gray.

My breasts were swollen, my skin burned, and because the entire dinner had felt like foreplay, I was more than a little ready for him from just his kiss and the anticipation. I tugged his shirt out of his suit trousers so I could slide my hand up under it to feel the smooth, hard— and sculpted!—hot skin against my palm. I groaned into his mouth and Gray's grip on my waist turned almost bruising. He sucked my tongue hard and I shuddered in need, eliciting a growl from him that turned the heat between us into wildfire.

Our kiss lost all control and I felt his warm, callused hands on my outer thighs as they brushed my skin, pushing my dress up to my waist. Gray curled his hands around the fabric of my knickers and tugged, breaking the kiss to stare into my eyes as he pulled them down. I felt them fall around my ankles and as cold air hit between my legs, my belly squeezed, causing another rush of wet.

I shivered with want as I kicked my underwear away. Gray's eyes were so dark they were almost black and his jaw was taut with tension. He brought his lips to mine but barely brushed them, staring deep into my eyes.

"Spread your legs, angel," he murmured against my mouth.

Another belly squeeze.

Holy crap.

I did as asked, my breath stuttering as Gray leaned one hand against the wall at my head and slid the other between my legs. His fingers pushed in, eased by my wetness, and as his thumb came down on my clit, his eyes flared and a groan rumbled out between his lips from somewhere deep inside him.

"Fuck," he grunted against my mouth. "Fuck, you're ready. So ready."

"That's what you do to me," I whispered on a gasp as his fingers moved inside me.

Gray dropped his hand from the wall as he kept pleasuring me with his other and he made short, jerky movements as he unbuttoned and unzipped his trousers. Then he took my hand and suddenly I had his hot, pulsing erection in it.

His eyes squeezed shut for a second as I fondled him and when they opened he stared deep into mine. "And that's what you do to me."

Suddenly we were kissing again—lips biting, nipping, licking, as we both reached to shove his trousers down. Then he broke the kiss to bend down to collect a condom from his back pocket. When he straightened to roll it down his straining arousal, I whimpered with need. He was unsurprisingly big… but he also had impressive girth too.

"Holy…" I breathed.

"All yours, angel." Gray flashed me a cocky grin that made me giggle—laughter that ended with a gasp as he gripped my legs, spread them, and thrust up into me.

"Oh God!" I cried out in pleasured shock, his throbbing heat overwhelming me. I wrapped my arms around his back, my fingers curling into the fabric of his shirt and the muscle beneath. Gray had one hand braced on the wall at my head and the other curled around my thigh, holding it against his waist as he powered in and out of me.

He'd lost control. This was fucking. Raw and hard.

And I was right there with him, glorying in the mind-blowing pleasure of it. Holding tight to him, I panted with excitement as he pounded us into the wall, thrusting into me hard, gliding in and out of my snug channel, each drive spurring us toward climax.

It didn't take long, my body had been so ready for him before he even entered me, and I blew apart.

"Ahhhh!" I cried out, shuddering and pulsing so hard it triggered Gray's release. He threw his head back, his eyes on me, his muscles strained as he let out a guttural grunt, my sex pulsing around him as he jerked inside me.

Gray's body melted against mine, his forehead dropping to my shoulder. "Fuck," he huffed.

I caressed his back, feeling it rise and fall as he tried to catch his breath. Attempting to catch my own, I could only nod.

He lifted his head to stare into my eyes. To my shock, I saw concern there. "That wasn't how I wanted our first time to go. You okay?"

I smiled lazily. "Babe, you just gave me the best orgasm of my life. I'm more than okay." I felt him pulse in little aftershocks inside me. "Gray," I whimpered.

His eyes flashed. "More?"

"More," I demanded, sliding my hand up his back to clasp his nape and draw his head to mine. My kiss was full of need.

I sighed into his mouth as he slid out of me.

Gray grunted and broke the kiss to huff, "Fuck, you're so goddamn sexy, I never want to let you out of my bed."

"We would have to eventually leave for sustenance."

"Screw that. Death by sex doesn't sound so bad," he teased.

I laughed and agreed, "Not the way you do it."

His eyes glinted with laughter as he said, "Did you notice we crossed off number seven on your list?"

Confused for a moment, I froze. "Number seven?"

"Your list today."

And then it dawned on me.

7. AHHHH!

I threw my head back in laughter, not missing the way Gray watched me with tenderness. When I finally stopped giggling, he cupped my face and pressed a sweet kiss to my lips. "Wait there while I deal with this condom. Bathroom?"

I pointed and he pulled up his trousers before striding over and into it. Feeling the shiver of want cascade over me, I knew I was nowhere near done with him. First I pulled my dress up and off and threw it on a nearby chair. My bra and sandals followed next.

Gray came back out of the bathroom, fully clothed, and stuttered to a stop at the sight of me waiting on him in the nude.

I felt every inch of my skin blush as he visually devoured me. When his gaze finally locked with mine, tears burned in the back of my eyes at the awe I found there. "I've never seen anything as fucking beautiful as you in my whole life, angel. And I've seen a lot of beauty."

My smile trembled with emotion and I took a step toward him. "Shirt off," I whispered.

He immediately obeyed, throwing it on the chair to join my dress. Gray made to take a step toward me but I shook my head. He frowned but stayed still and I loved him for it.

I loved him.

I *loved* him.

How that could be I didn't know, but it was true.

Grinning at my little (or big!) secret, I strolled toward him with an exaggerated swing in my hips that made my breasts bounce, and Gray's eyes turned molten. As soon as I stopped before him, my body almost flush with his, he reached up to cup my breasts in his large hands, swiping my nipples with his thumbs. Sensation flooded through me, heading straight between my legs and I dropped my head back as he touched and caressed and squeezed my breasts. My own hands roamed his hard chest, my thumbs brushing his nipples, exploring him in a way I'd wanted to from that first night in the bar.

Then suddenly his mouth was on me, tonguing and sucking my nipples until I was whimpering and moaning with need.

It took me some time to find my way out of the fog and it was with much reluctance that I pressed my hands to his shoulders to push him back.

He scowled impatiently at me and I had to bite my lip to stop from smiling. "My turn to cross something off my list."

Gray's eyebrows furrowed and this time I grinned. "Number eight." I slid my hand down his hard, beautiful stomach and rubbed the heel of my palm over his zipper where his erection aggressively strained. Up on tip-toes, my hard nipples brushing his chest, I leaned in to whisper in his ear, "I suck."

Somehow, he got even harder under my hand and when I pulled back his whole face was taut with need. I watched him—unbelievably turned on by how much he wanted me—as I unzipped his trousers and released him.

When I lowered to my knees in front of him I swear to God his eyes almost rolled into the back of his head before my mouth even got near him.

* * * *

Gray's lips moved down my stomach, his tongue licking my belly button before moving further down. My lower belly rippled in a mini-orgasm as his mouth got closer to where I wanted it the most.

After I took him to heaven in my mouth, Gray had undressed completely, and then we'd made love on the big four poster bed in my suite. We'd dozed for a while until I'd become fully alert at the feel of Gray's mouth on my breast. And now he was making it clear he was about to offer his own oral gift in return for mine earlier.

My legs fell open, inviting him in, and I heard his grunt of satisfaction seconds before his tongue touched my clit.

Want slammed through me and my hips pushed into his mouth. He gripped them, pressing them back to the mattress, and he started to destroy me in the best way possible. He suckled my clit, pulling on it hard, and as I began to undulate against his mouth, Gray stopped.

I made an incoherent noise of frustration and felt a puff of breath against me that suggested he'd just laughed.

"Gray," I begged.

He gave me his tongue back, this time licking inside me. I writhed because it wasn't enough. I needed more.

Hearing my whimpers, Gray returned to my clit, let go of my left hip and gently pushed two fingers inside of me. I was so swollen and sensitive, it was the most intense kind of pleasure burn.

"Gray." I bucked against him as he used both his mouth and fingers to push me to climax.

And then he stopped again. Just as I was about to explode.

"No!" I gasped in frustration.

And so it went, Gray bringing me close to coming and then stopping.

"Gray, please," I whimpered, feeling tears of desire thicken my throat.

At the sound of my emotional plea, he suddenly braced over me, his hand on my inner thigh, pushing me open as his other pressed into the mattress at my shoulder. He brushed his lips over mine. "I'll take care of you, angel. I'll always take care of you." He quickly reached for one of the two condoms he'd dropped on the bedside table earlier, thankfully took seconds to put it on, and then he eased inside of me. One glide, two, and that was all it took.

I shattered around him and Gray kept pumping slowly in and out. His expression darkened and tensed with need as he controlled his thrusts and just watching him move over me, beautiful and strong, feeling his thick hardness inside of me, got me hot all over again. I gasped in wonder as that familiar need coiled tightly low in my belly and Gray's eyes flared with understanding.

"Come, Autumn," he growled. "I'm not coming until you come again."

I wrapped my legs around his waist and curled my fingernails into his taut, delicious arse. His thrusts came harder, faster. "Yes, yes!"

"Oh fuck, angel, come, you gotta come."

His wish, my command.

I blew apart.

Gray's deep shout of pleasure filled my suite as his hips jerked against mine. He collapsed over me and I wrapped myself around him, luxuriating in the feel of his shuddering body as he came down from his climax.

Holy shit.

Who knew?

Not wanting to crush me, Gray rolled to his side, and we clung to each other. He was still inside me. We kissed. Slowly. Languidly. Sweetly.

"I didn't know," I whispered. "I didn't know it could be like this."

His hold on me tightened. "Me neither."

We lay there in silence, just gazing into each other's eyes, in wonder. I hadn't known it was possible to lie with a man like this, to feel so unbelievably connected in every way.

"Number nine," Gray eventually whispered.

9. HOLD ME :(

"I need to turn that sad face upside down though," I whispered back, smiling.

"And add the word 'forever.'" He rested his forehead against mine. "I'm going to hold you forever, Autumn O'Dea."

A tear slipped down my cheek before I could stop it and Gray caught it on his thumb. He pulled back to stare at me in concern and I shook my head. "Happy tears," I promised.

Tenderness swept over his expression and was quickly replaced by something I didn't understand until he kissed me.

It was a possessive kiss, deep and hungry, and demanding.

That and his look told me what he didn't say.

I belonged to him.

And he belonged to me.

As we lay in each other's arms, wrapped tight and warm and safe, I tried my best to push away my fears… because we still hadn't addressed one big blue problem. That bloody great big ocean between us.

Chapter Seven

Gray had ski lessons booked for that morning so he had to leave my bed to shower and change. I loved how reluctant he was to go, peppering every inch of me with kisses.

"If you don't stop I'm going to make you late," I warned, smiling dreamily at the ceiling, my fingers curled in his thick, soft hair as he trailed kisses across my stomach. My hands slipped down his head to his back as he came over me and kissed me.

"Unfortunately, I really have to go." He gave me another quick kiss and then rolled out of bed.

I turned onto my side to enjoy the view as he crossed the room to where his clothes were piled on the chair. The man had the finest arse I'd ever seen in my life. I wanted to bite it.

He turned as he dressed and caught me leering. Laughing, he shook his head. "Stop it."

I grinned. "I can't help it. You're delicious."

Looking pleased that I thought so, he quickly shrugged on his shirt and began to button it. "I'm booked until one. You want to do lunch?"

"Definitely. I told Susan and Molly I'd go over to their place at nine o' clock to go over things and see where the plans are at. The party is in three days. I'll need your kitchen the day before that."

"No problem, angel." He came back over the bed and leaned down to give me one last lingering kiss. "Best night of my life."

Joy suffused me and I felt weirdly, stupidly shy all of a sudden. "Me, too."

"Christ, you're adorable." Another kiss. "Right, I gotta go or I just won't." He pushed away from me and stepped back, his eyes dipping down my body. Gray let out a regretful sigh before he returned his gaze to mine. "I'll come find you at Susan's condo when I'm done."

"Can't wait."

When he did leave, the sound of my suite door closing with a click echoing around the large space, I felt a pang in my chest.

I missed him already.

How weird was that?

Knowing if I lazed around in bed, I'd just miss him more, I forced myself to get up and out of it and stumbled into the shower. It was while I was in the shower that I realized I hadn't looked at my phone since yesterday afternoon. Shit. What if Killian had called? It didn't go off last night in the suite so maybe he hadn't. As soon as I got out of the shower I searched for the damn phone and found it buried under my dress on the chair. It was off, having run out of charge.

Damn.

Worry flooded me. How long had it been dead and had Killian been trying to reach me?

I plugged it into the charger and waited impatiently for it to come on. After a few minutes, my stomach sank as I watched message after message and missed call after missed call come up on the screen.

Some were from Killian, others from Skylar, and there was a missed call and text from Catie.

I quickly shot a text to Catie to tell her I was fine and I'd see her at breakfast to explain. Then I called Killian.

"Hey, big brother," I greeted him cheerfully when he answered, in the hopes that my good mood would soften him.

There was a moment of silence and then what sounded like whispering and then, "Hey, Autumn, you've got Skylar."

Although happy to hear Skylar's voice, I frowned. "Hey, Sky, what's up?"

Her voice lowered. "Your brother just handed me the phone and wandered off, brooding."

Concern pierced me. "My phone died. Is he mad at me?"

"A little, I think. He tried calling you last night and when you didn't answer he got worried, so he called Catie and she told him you were out on a date?"

Since she asked it like a question I answered as such, "Yes, I was on a date."

Nervous butterflies fluttered to life in my belly.

"Killian's just a little worried."

"That I'm dating?"

"Um… yes."

Irritation flooded me. I was the happiest I'd ever been and I didn't really feel like explaining myself to my brother. "Well, tell him he has no reason to be."

Skylar was quiet a moment. "So… who's the guy?"

My smile was automatic and I sank down onto the edge of the bed. "Skylar… oh man, Skylar, I can't even describe him."

She sounded amused, "You sound… dreamy?"

I giggled. "I do, don't I?"

"Are you drunk?" she laughed.

"On love," I admitted.

It surprised me for a second that I'd said it out loud but only a second. I'd always been an open book but there were some things even I kept to myself. Not with Skylar. I couldn't explain why but from the moment we met I'd been able to tell her anything. She didn't judge people. Skylar was thoughtful, empathetic, and understanding.

And so I found myself telling her all about Gray and our instant connection. About how I couldn't explain it but it was real… "I'm in love with him."

She was silent so long, tears began to burn in my throat. Tears of regret. I shouldn't have told her. How could anyone but Gray and me understand?

"You think I'm being an idiot," I whispered.

"God, no," Skylar replied immediately. "Autumn, I know you've had bad luck with guys in the past but that was not your fault. You're sweet and kind and you treat everyone like your best friend, but you are also smart and capable. You're not a dreamer with your head up your ass… so if you say you think you're in love with this guy then I believe you."

Relief flooded me. "Really?"

"Yes. But that doesn't mean I'm not concerned. I don't like that it's happened so quickly and that it's with someone neither I nor Killian has even met. But you can't blame me for feeling that way."

"No, I get it." And I did. If Killian had fallen in love with Skylar without me having met her I'd have worried, not liking the idea of him investing emotionally in someone I didn't know or like. "How do you think Killian will react?"

She sighed. "I think you know how he'll react. He's not just your big brother. He's *parent* and big brother. He's not going to like this."

And that put a big fat dampener on it.

"Have you thought about how this relationship is going to work with you here and your guy in Montana?"

There was the other big fat dampener.

"No," I answered honestly. "I haven't."

"Autumn, please be careful. I'm not saying what you're feeling isn't real but this is a complicated situation. Maybe take some time to work all that stuff out before you get in any deeper with this guy."

"Gray doesn't want to talk about it just yet. He said he wants our hooks so deep in each other we'll do anything to figure it out."

Skylar let out a huff of laughter. "I bet he did."

"How's that?" I frowned.

"Babe, you've seen *you*, right? You're drop dead gorgeous, confident without vanity, and just the sweetest, nicest person you could meet. I bet your guy took one look at you and decided he'd do and say just about anything to make you his and to make you stay. That's what he means by doing anything to figure it out. I bet he wants you to move there."

Unease settled over me. "You think?"

"He owns a successful construction company there. He has a big loving family. He wants to take you hiking in the summer." Wow, she'd really listened to everything I told her. "This is not a guy who wants to leave Montana."

"But I don't want to leave Glasgow." And I didn't. "I've never been away from Killian for more than a few weeks." He was my family.

"Then you really need to talk to your guy before you fall any harder."

Emotion clogged my throat. I sounded hoarse when I retorted, "I don't think I can fall any harder. I'm already there." I sucked in a shaky, teary breath. "What am I going to do?"

"You need to talk to him. And then you need to call me to let me know you're okay. Do you want me to tell Killian?"

I knew it was cowardly to ask her to, but I just couldn't handle my brother's feelings on top of my own right then. "Would you? It'll just make it easier for me when I do finally talk to him about it."

"Of course."

Needing to shake myself out of my dark thoughts, I changed the subject. "I've commandeered this whole conversation. How are you doing?"

Skylar released a heavy sigh. "I don't feel so jetlagged anymore and I'm nervous because the press has backed off entirely just in time for us dropping the album. So I know they'll be back, even though I refuse to promote it."

"The album is amazing. It's going to soar."

"You know I don't care about that. And without marketing it's doubtful. But it's my best work ever and I just wanted to put it out there."

"I think you're going to be surprised," I said, genuinely believing that this album would rock the charts and get millions of streams.

"We'll see."

We talked some more about her plans for the album drop and I told her about Susan and Molly.

"Only you, Autumn," she said, the fondness in her voice unmistakable. "You go on vacation and then end up helping people out."

"It's not entirely altruistic. It's Gray's plan to help me work out what I want to do with my life."

"And how's that working out for you?"

"Hmm... he's proving something of a distraction, but I'm leaning toward event management." And I was. I think I was even before the list.

"Good. Look, I better go. I can hear your brother playing something moody and melancholic on the guitar and I need to put him in a better mood before I drop your news on him."

I wrinkled my nose. "TMI."

"I didn't say *how* I was going to put him in a better mood."

"You didn't have to. Anyway, you go do something I'm going to pretend you and my brother don't do, and I'm going to get dressed and head down to breakfast. I'm starved." And I was. A long night of sex would do that to a girl.

"Okay. Love you, babe."

"Love you, too, Sky. And tell my brother I love him."

"You got it."

We hung up and I got dressed for the day, trying to ignore the churn of worry in my gut. That feeling wasn't just about how Killian would react to the news of Gray, but also about my future with Gray. Skylar was right. Gray would in no way want to leave Cunningham Falls. What the hell was I supposed to do with that? I couldn't move to Montana.

Could I?

The thought of being so far away from Killian and Skylar caused a painful ache in my chest I just couldn't ignore. Killian had been my only family for so long and I, more than anyone, knew how important family was and how fragile life could be. I didn't want to miss out on the important moments in Killian's life and I didn't want him to miss out on mine. I wanted to be there after he proposed to Skylar, to be a bridesmaid at their wedding, to cradle my niece or nephew at Skylar's bedside, and babysit for them when they needed alone time.

And I wanted Killian and Skylar to be there for me when I went through all of those moments with Gray. Because, as crazy as it was, I couldn't imagine sharing those moments with anyone else but Gray.

Heartbreakingly, I couldn't imagine *not* sharing those moments with my brother and the woman he loved. It would put me in the middle of an ocean being emotionally pulled in opposite directions. I'd have to either swim in one direction, leaving someone behind, or I'd drown.

* * * *

"Oh, Autumn." Catie reached over the table to squeeze my free hand while I wiped the corner of my eyes with the napkin in my other.

I blinked back tears, mortified I was getting upset at breakfast in public.

Catie and Kyle had taken one look at my face when I approached their table that morning and had known something was really wrong.

"I'm being silly and melodramatic," I huffed, throwing Kyle a look of apology.

"You're not," Catie assured me. "But I think Skylar is right. You need to talk to Gray before this goes any further."

I sniffled and wiped at my eyes again. "Has my mascara—" My words fell away at the sight of Gray marching across the breakfast room, scowling.

"Why are you crying?" he said without preamble.

Shocked that he was there and had witnessed said crying, I could only stare at him. Then I blurted, "I thought you were skiing."

His frown deepened. "I have an hour between my first two lessons, thought I'd see if I could catch you and have breakfast, and gotta say, angel, not liking I'm finding you here in tears after last night." He flicked a look at Catie and Kyle then returned his gaze to mine. "Can we talk?"

I threw my friends a reassuring but wobbly smile and got up from the table. Gray immediately clasped my hand tight in his and led me out of the dining room. He turned left toward the restrooms where there was a mobile coat rack in the hallway. He gently nudged me behind it and pressed me up against the wall, not only securing some privacy for us, but overwhelming me in a possessive, macho man way that felt a little too much at the moment. He braced an arm on the wall beside my head and rested his other hand on my waist.

"Gray." I pressed against his chest but he only eased back a little.

"Crying, needing space. Yeah, not liking this at all. I left you smiling and happy in bed this morning. What the fuck happened after I left?"

I bit my lip. "I… I started to think about the future."

"Yeah, so?" He squeezed my waist. "What's the problem?"

"You want to stay in Montana. I want to stay in Scotland."

There. It was out there.

Gray studied my face for a moment and I couldn't miss the concern that flickered in his eyes. Finally he asked, "Would you consider staying here… at all?"

"I can't leave my brother, Gray. He's the only family I've ever had and I don't want to miss out on all the important moments in his life or vice versa. If something were to happen to him and I'd missed out on all of that… I'd have to live with so much regret. And it's not just that. I mean, Killian hasn't even met you. What if you don't get along or he's upset that this is happening so fast?"

For some reason that caused Gray's expression to darken and he stepped back from me entirely. Moments ago I'd felt overwhelmed by him and now that he was giving me space, I didn't like it. And I really didn't like it when he practically growled, "If you plan to make decisions about our future based on what your brother thinks about us, we've got even bigger problems than a location issue, babe."

Okay, so I was definitely 'angel' when he liked me and 'babe' when I'd pissed him off. Noted.

Also, I *hated* pissing him off.

But I was also a little pissed off he was being insensitive. "You're coming at this from your perspective, Gray. Big, boisterous loving family—parents, brother, cousins, aunts, and uncles. I only have Killian."

"Yeah, I get that. But I'm close to my brother, too. However, what you don't see is me waiting to see if Noah *approves* of you before I decide to make you a part of my future. You are my future. Period. The fact that I'm not that to you until I have your brother's approval fucking pisses me off."

Now I was really angry. My face flushed and his eyes narrowed at whatever he saw in my gaze. "Don't you understand why I'm so upset? I *have* decided you're my future. All those important moments I was talking about? I can't picture them now with anyone else but you and the reason I'm upset is because I want to share those moments, our moments, with my family who happens to be my brother and I'm scared shitless because whatever happens here"—I gestured frantically between us—"I'm going to lose someone that I love!"

The word rang out around us for just a fraction of a second and then Gray was kissing me.

He was kissing me like the only way to get oxygen was to kiss it out of me.

I wrapped myself around him, completely forgetting where we were.

When he finally pulled back, he said, sounding breathless, "You love me?"

I shrugged, helplessly. "Heart on sleeve girl here."

"You love me?"

"I love you."

He crushed me against him, holding me so tight. "I love you, too. Fuck, I love you, too."

I shook my head against his chest, feeling a spectacularly confusing rush of bliss and fear. "What are we doing, Gray?"

After a moment of just holding me, Gray tipped my head back with his thumb against my chin, and butterflies rushed to life in my belly at the way he looked at me. All barriers were down.

He loved me.

It blazed out of his eyes.

Gray *loved* me.

"I don't want to lose you," I whispered fearfully.

Shaking his head, he hushed me. "Let's just sit on it for a few days, okay? We'll each take time to think, to really think, all the while enjoying the fuck out of loving each other. And when your vacation is coming to an end, we'll sit down and we'll hash this out. But whatever happens, Autumn, you won't lose someone you love. So I'm asking you to just hold on a few more days. Can you do that? Can you hold on?"

I nodded, knowing there wasn't much I wouldn't do for this man. "I can hold on."

Chapter Eight

As promised, I only considered our dilemma when we weren't enjoying the heck out of each other. And we did. Oh, we did that thoroughly.

I'd never considered myself particularly sexually adventurous before Gray, but when I was with him all my inhibitions disappeared. No man had ever made me feel more wanted and that gave me a kind of sexual confidence and power that made me revel in our lovemaking.

When we weren't sequestered in my suite, I was with Susan and Molly putting together the finishing touches for Molly's party. Most of our invites had been responded to within twenty-four hours and I'd organized a large bus to collect Molly's friends and family and bring them up Whitetail Mountain. Thanks to Gray, those who wanted to receive ski rental equipment and free lessons could—something he'd worked out with the owner, Jacob, so it wouldn't eat into my budget.

Molly and Susan were surrounded by supportive friends and family who seemed relieved to see the two enjoying themselves. I'd decorated the condo with fairy lights, pink and white paper floral arrangements in amongst the real ones, and strands of rose gold bunting.

The day before, Gray had let me loose in his kitchen in the condo but the problem was, for some reason, my baking turned him on. He kept distracting and interrupting me with his hands and mouth.

While my cupcakes were cooling, he'd unzipped both our jeans and fucked me on the kitchen counter. There was no other word for it.

And it was glorious!

Gray appeared at the party to be there when I gave Molly her gift from me and him—a necklace I'd seen her admiring in Dress It Up. She was delighted and after receiving a hug from Gray that made her get this soft, dreamy look on her face, Gray left us to it. Not without first telling me he'd see me later, with a sensual promise in his beautiful eyes.

The party was a huge success and my appetizers and baked goods went down an absolute treat. Having promised to keep some for Gray, I managed to snag a cupcake, fairy cake, and a couple of brownies before they were all gone. With them secured in a small airtight container in my hands, I waved a final goodbye to Susan and Molly after a tearful cluster of hugs.

I'd given Susan my number and email and asked her to keep me up to date but only if she felt like it. The truth was I was melancholy leaving them because I wanted everything to turn out all right for them, and it was just one of those horrible occasions when it never really would. I knew because I'd been through it. You moved on with your life but it was always just that little bit empty. That was what it was to be human. To keep living, to find happiness, but doing it always being just that little bit sad because loss was inevitable.

I crossed the car park toward the lodge, toward Gray, knowing that I'd lose him eventually. But I didn't want it to be now, or tomorrow, or ten years from now, or even fifty.

I wanted it to be after a lifetime of happiness together, when its inevitability was natural and right, and we were hopefully holding hands in bed together in our nineties, drifting off peacefully in our sleep.

Hurrying, I almost slipped, and marveled that it was my first almost graceless fall since I'd collided with Gray on the slopes. And oh, what a story to tell our kids! That Mummy took Daddy down on a ski slope, then accidentally kneed him in the junk and thankfully won his heart despite that.

I didn't know how it would work but I couldn't wait to tell Gray that it *was* going to work.

Catching sight of Jeanette at reception, I practically rushed her to ask if she'd seen Gray.

She grinned knowingly at me. Everyone at the lodge knew about our romance. It would have been a miracle if they didn't, considering we spent almost every available second attached at the hip.

"He told me to tell you he has the infinity pool all to himself, if you want to join him there."

A tingle awakened between my legs just at the thought. What a treat. The heated jacuzzi pool was small, half-moon shaped, and built into a balcony that jutted out from the lodge over the mountains. When you sat in it and stared out of the edge, you felt like you were floating over the snow.

I had never moved so fast in my life, hurrying back to my room to change into my bikini and robe. Not forgetting the baked goods, I practically sprinted to the spa, which had a closed sign on it, and slipped inside. It was weird being there when it was empty, but Gray had left some lighting on for me, lighting that acted as a guide toward the outdoor area.

The balcony was dimly light and I saw his silhouette in the pool. He had his arms crossed on the ledge, staring thoughtfully out at the mountains. I opened the door, drawing his gaze, and made quick work of slipping out of my robe and slippers and lowering myself into the heat of the pool, out of the freezing cold air. I grabbed the cakes off the ground and bobbed toward him with the container in my hand.

Gray grinned, reaching an arm out to pull me toward him. He relieved me of the container with his other.

"How did you swing this?" I asked.

"Jacob gave me the key. Though he said if we had sex in this pool he'd kill me."

I burst out laughing, and it was soon muffled in Gray's long, luxurious kiss. I smiled as we settled at the edge of the pool and he opened the container.

Watching in delight and anticipation as he bit into my frosted cupcake, I leaned closer for his reaction. His gaze flicked to me as he ate and made a 'yummy' face. I grinned harder. After he swallowed he said, "Angel, fuck, you can bake."

"That's just a cupcake. Wait until you taste my chocolate hazelnut cake."

His eyes lit at the prospect.

And I continued, my breath puffing in the cold air between us, "And you will. I hope you'll be tasting my cakes until we're old and decrepit."

Gray was about to take another bite of cupcake but stopped.

Instead his mouth formed a gorgeous, crooked smile. "You mean that?"

"I mean that. I don't know how we're going to do it but we have to find a way."

"Six months in Montana, six months in Scotland," he offered immediately. "Best of both worlds."

Tears of happiness immediately rushed my eyes before I could stop them. "You'd do that?"

"If you'll do it for me, I'll do it for you. And it's not like it's a hardship, angel. If Scotland's half as beautiful as you, I'll be happy."

I threw my arms around him, knocking the container out of his hand and into the water, but I didn't care. Kissing the life out of him, tasting cupcake and frosting, I knew I'd never been happier in my whole life. I didn't think it was possible to be this ecstatic.

His arms closed tight around me and soon our kiss turned to more. His hands were everywhere, cupping and caressing my breasts, sliding between my legs.

"You're on the pill, right?"

"Right," I murmured in a sex haze. "But why?"

"I'm clean. You?"

"Hmm, yeah, why?"

He nudged my bikini bottoms out of the way and suddenly thrust inside me. I gasped in pleasure and shock.

"I thought... no sex," I panted.

"Angel, there's cupcake and brownie crap all over the bottom of this pool. If it needs to be cleaned anyway..." He pumped into me harder to make his point.

And that night we made a memory I'll never forget. Gray making love to me with the dark snowy Montana mountain as our backdrop. We came together, in a harmony that fit the moment perfectly and as I clung to the man I loved, he brushed his lips against my ear and whispered, "You owe me a cupcake."

I laughed because he was funny... but mostly because that's all I ever wanted to do now that he was mine. Love, sex, laugh.

Heaven.

Epilogue

Snow Ghost Lodge
Eighteen Months Later

It was August, the slopes were closed and wouldn't open until skiing season restarted in November, but the stunning Snow Ghost Lodge was open to a private event.

A small but beautifully organized wedding. Even if, as the wedding planner, I did say so myself.

Since it was *my* wedding I could get away with it.

I thought I'd feel nervous on my wedding day but my butterflies were excited ones because I couldn't wait to change my name to Autumn King. Couldn't. Freaking. Wait!

The last eighteen months had been a challenge but one that Gray and I overcame with the ease of two people who loved each other enough to make anything work. I'd extended my holiday by a week in Montana to meet his parents and his brother Noah. Thankfully, they liked me. Like a lot. It came as no surprise that Gray's family was as loving as he was.

The hard part came when Gray decided to come back to Scotland with me to meet Killian and Skylar.

Killian did not make it easy at first, but he soon came to admire Gray's straight-talking. He pretty much told Killian in front of me and Skylar that he loved me, I loved him, and if Killian loved me as much as he was supposed to he'd get over his shit and give Gray a chance.

It was exactly the right thing to say to my brother and thanks to Skylar, who had turned him into a romantic even if he wouldn't admit it, Killian gave Gray a chance. We stayed for a month before it was time to head back to Montana for Gray's work. During that month Killian proposed to Skylar and I was content in the knowledge that I didn't miss out on that moment.

However, the idea of me moving to the US did not go down well with Killian. In fact, our relationship became a little strained when I moved to Montana. Gray had to work overtime to help me adjust to my new life.

I busied myself setting up my new event management company—something that was not easy to get off the ground but I worked my arse off and with a little help from Susan and word of mouth, I started to get work and my portfolio began to grow. Skylar got Killian on a plane and they spent a month with us that May. They flew over a couple more times during the summer and between that and video chatting I didn't feel like I was missing out too badly. Over time, Killian realized the depth of Gray's love for me and that he had a good family who showed me a lot of love, too, and the strain between us disappeared.

Come November, Gray and I flew back to Glasgow but we didn't stay for six months. I had my company now and so did Gray, and the truth was that Killian and Skylar could move to Timbuktu and I'd never lose them. No matter where we were, we had each other.

Gray and I stayed in Glasgow all through Christmas (something that didn't go down well with his family and was one of the aforementioned challenges we had to face) and the month of January. In early February, I stood beside Skylar as her maid of honor as she and Killian married in secret in Loch Lomond. Only me, Gray, our friend Eve who used to work for Killian, Skylar's ex bandmates Brandon and Austin and their respective dates, and her manager Gayle attended. Her other ex-bandmate and just plain old ex, Micah, declined to attend for obvious reasons.

The press didn't find out about their marriage until four weeks later when Skylar and Killian were spotted by paparazzi in Los Angeles wearing wedding bands.

After my brother's private wedding, Gray and I headed home to the US. Gray got in some skiing time before the slopes closed and I returned to planning events, including our own wedding.

I should note that Gray proposed to me the day after we arrived back in Montana a year before Skylar and Killian's wedding. Of course I said yes, but while Gray wanted to get married right away, I wanted my brother to be truly happy for me before I asked him to walk me down the aisle.

I needed him to know he was doing the right thing by giving me away to Gray.

Gray understood but it still annoyed him and he wasn't good at hiding his impatience for the next sixteen months.

Turning to look up at my brother as the entrance song started up beyond the double doors, I squeezed his arm. "You look nervous. You know you're doing the right thing."

Killian stared down at me. To the outside world his expression seemed remote. But I saw a million emotions in the dark brown eyes so like my own. "I know," he said, his voice low, hoarse. "I'd have kidnapped you and taken you back to Glasgow by now if I didn't know that." He covered my beautifully manicured hand resting on his arm. "No one deserves you, kid. No one. But Gray comes pretty damn close. That'll just have to do for me."

I smiled through happy tears. "I love you, big brother."

Watching him fight emotion, he nodded, his reply gruff, "Love you more."

The doors swung open slowly, revealing the dining room now turned into a ceremony room. We hadn't invited tons of guests, just friends and family from Cunningham Falls and a few from back home in Glasgow.

Every third chair on either side of the aisle was decorated with a white candle in a modern, square lantern. They echoed the simplicity of the rest of the décor. Soft, elegant, and earthy. At the top of the aisle I saw the officiant and Skylar and Catie in different bridesmaid gowns in the same color of cobalt blue to match Gray's eyes. Their dresses also matched the groom's and his best man's bow ties.

Gray's brother, Noah, stood at his side but my eyes only flickered to him before they moved back to my husband-to-be.

I would never forget the way he looked in his tux, not just because he was sexy as heck, but because of the expression in his eyes as he wore it watching my brother walk me down the aisle toward him.

A few years ago I'd witnessed my brother fall in love with Skylar

Finch and, as happy as I was for them both, I'd felt sad for myself because I never believed I'd find a man who looked at me the way Killian looked at Skylar.

But Fate had smiled on me when I decided to go on the last trip I'd ever thought I'd take—a skiing trip!

Wearing a pair of skis, I'd knocked Gray on his arse, literally, and only a few hours later, in his words, I'd done it wearing a pair of sky-high heels, only this time it was figuratively. Emotionally.

Gray didn't look at me like Killian looked at Skylar. He couldn't. Their love was theirs, ours was ours. He looked at me in a different way but it made me feel how I hoped Skylar felt when Killian looked at her.

It made me feel like the only woman in the world worth looking at.

It made me feel like *I* was Gray's entire world.

It made me feel that way because I *was* his entire world.

And he was mine.

Killian had barely brought us to the bottom of the aisle when Gray stepped forward to impatiently claim me. My brother rolled his eyes but released me to take his seat, and I laughed softly as Gray pulled me into him.

I had to hold my bouquet out to Skylar without turning to her because Gray wouldn't let me go. And as we said our vows in front of our friends and family in the room I'd walked into all those months ago, catching Gray's heart without even saying a word, I knew he never would.

* * * *

"Gray, where are we going?" I laughed as I practically had to run to keep up with him, the skirt of my wedding dress clutched tightly in my free hand.

He didn't answer.

"Gray? We have photos to take and guests to keep entertained while they turn the ceremony room back into a dining room!"

Suddenly he stopped, catching me against him as I stumbled in my blue Jimmy Choos. "Gray!"

He flashed me a wicked grin and swiped a room key over the door we'd stopped in front of.

It was my old suite. The suite we'd booked for our wedding night.

"Gray, no!" But it was too late.

I found myself hauled into the room, and the door slammed shut behind us. He clasped me to him and kissed the life out of me as I tried to offer protest. It was a feeble attempt and he knew it as he pushed me up against the wall and fumbled under my skirts.

"We can't do this. This is for later," I moaned between kisses. "Guests, Gray."

"Angel, you want me sporting wood in our wedding photos?"

"Negatory."

"That's what I thought," he mumbled, pressing kisses down my neck as he peeled my knickers down under my dress. "And the only way to solve that problem is to fuck my wife." He growled after he said that. "My wife. Jesus, that sounds good."

Apparently very good because our first time together as husband and wife happened right there, against the wall, in the exact same spot we first had sex.

I was really enjoying the symmetry of our wedding.

Flushing as Gray helped me get cleaned and straightened up, I shook my head at him. "Everyone will know where we went and why."

He shrugged, taking hold of my hand to lead me back out of the suite. "Who cares? Let them know. You know what I know?"

"What?" I asked as he wrapped his arm around me to draw me into his side.

"What we have is fucking beautiful. Not in my life did I ever think I'd love or need or want my wife as much as I love, need, and want you. You'd been unlucky, angel, for a long time, but it never stopped you from taking a gamble on life. You gambled on me when you promised me you'd keep holding on. And you gotta know by now that I'm going to make sure that gamble pays off and pays off good every day for the rest of your life."

I slid my hand up his chest to caress his cheek. "You should have said that in your vows."

"No. No one gets that but you." He kissed me, not having to lower his head since I was wearing my standard five-inch heels. Not surprisingly with how raw our emotions were, the kiss turned hungry.

"Oh for Christ sake." My brother's voice interrupted us and we pulled apart to find him standing up ahead with his arms crossed over his chest. He glared at Gray. "Can you keep your hands off my wee sister long enough to let the photographer take usable photos?"

Gray smirked, leading us toward Killian. "My wife."

"Excuse me?"

"My wife."

Understanding, Killian scowled. "She's still my wee sister."

"Not when my tongue's in her mouth," Gray replied with no small amount of smugness.

I burst out laughing at Killian's affronted expression and grabbed his arm to lead the three of us back toward our guests and photographer. "You walked into that one, Kill."

He harrumphed but his expression softened as he studied me. "You look happy."

"Bliss," I replied, beaming.

My brother's gaze drifted from my face to across the room as we walked back through the double doors to the ceremony/dining room. His dark eyes stopped on Skylar, who turned upon our entrance. She looked stunning in blue. And Killian's gaze said he thought so, too. As their eyes held, their expressions said a lot more than that.

"Aye," he murmured and I knew it was in response to what I'd said.

And that made my joy even more joyful, knowing he felt that way about Skylar.

Killian and I may have had it easy financially, but everything else in life that actually mattered was something we'd fought for. Love had not been easy for either of us and we'd both lived with a loneliness that unfortunately our love for one another could never really take away.

Yet here we were with our soul mates and luckier than most people ever got to be.

All because we decided to hold on.

And hold on tight.

Killian let go of me to walk across the room to Skylar, drawing her into his arms as she chatted animatedly with Catie and Kyle. She wrapped hers around his and leaned back into his chest.

I turned into my husband, catching sight of the photographer heading toward us out of the corner of my eyes and grinned up at him as I recalled words he'd said to me when we first discussed the amazing, wondrous connection between us. "Someone needs to discover the formula and bottle this shit so everyone can get a piece of the good life."

Gray's eyes brightened and I knew he remembered when he gave my waist an answering squeeze. "You're lucky you're sweet and beautiful, angel, or this next part would be torture."

Suffice it to say that for such a handsome specimen of man, Gray did not like getting his photograph taken. We turned as the photographer caught up to us and I murmured so only my husband could hear, "It'll be over before you know it. Just hold on."

He turned to me. I knew in that moment I was the only person in the room as he promised, "Always, angel. Always."

THE END

Sign up for the 1001 Dark Nights Newsletter
and be entered to win a Tiffany Lock necklace.

There's a contest every quarter!

Go to www.1001DarkNights.com to subscribe.

As a bonus, all subscribers can download
FIVE FREE exclusive books!

Discover the Kristen Proby Crossover Collection

Soaring with Fallon: A Big Sky Novel
By Kristen Proby

Fallon McCarthy has climbed the corporate ladder. She's had the office with the view, the staff, and the plaque on her door. The unexpected loss of her grandmother taught her that there's more to life than meetings and conference calls, so she quit, and is happy to be a nomad, checking off items on her bucket list as she takes jobs teaching yoga in each place she lands in. She's happy being free, and has no interest in being tied down.

When Noah King gets the call that an eagle has been injured, he's not expecting to find a beautiful stranger standing vigil when he arrives. Rehabilitating birds of prey is Noah's passion, it's what he lives for, and he doesn't have time for a nosy woman who's suddenly taken an interest in Spread Your Wings sanctuary.

But Fallon's gentle nature, and the way she makes him laugh, and *feel* again draws him in. When it comes time for Fallon to move on, will Noah's love be enough for her to stay, or will he have to find the strength to let her fly?

* * * *

Wicked Force: A Wicked Horse Vegas/Big Sky Novella
By Sawyer Bennett

From *New York Times* and *USA Today* bestselling author Sawyer Bennett...

Joslyn Meyers has taken the celebrity world by storm, drawing the attention of millions. But one fan's affections has gone too far, and she's running to the one place she hopes he'll never find her – back home to Cunningham Falls.

Kynan McGrath leads The Jameson Group, a world-class security organization, and he's ready to do what it takes to keep Joslyn safe, even if it means giving up his own life in return. The one thing he's not prepared to lose, though, is his heart.

* * * *

Crazy Imperfect Love: A Dirty Dicks/Big Sky Novella
By KL Grayson

From *USA Today* bestselling author KL Grayson...

Abigail Darwin needs one thing in life: consistency. Okay, make that two things: consistency and order. Tired of being shackled to her obsessive-compulsive mind, Abigail is determined to break free. Which is why she's shaking things up.

Fresh out of nursing school, she takes a traveling nurse position. A new job in a new city every few months? That's a sure-fire way to keep her from settling down and falling into old habits. First stop, Cunningham Falls, Montana.

The only problem? She didn't plan on falling in love with the quaint little town, and she sure as heck didn't plan on falling for its resident surgeon, Dr. Drake Merritt

Laid back, messy, and spontaneous, Drake is everything she's not. But he is completely smitten by the new, quirky nurse working on the med-surg floor of the hospital.

Abby puts up a good fight, but Drake is determined to break through her carefully erected walls to find out what makes her tick. And sigh and moan and smile and laugh. Because he really loves her laugh.

But falling in love isn't part of Abby's plan. Will Drake have what it takes to convince her that the best things in life come from doing what scares us the most?

* * * *

Worth Fighting For: A Warrior Fight Club/Big Sky Novella
By Laura Kaye

From *New York Times* and *USA Today* bestselling author Laura Kaye...

Getting in deep has never felt this good...

Commercial diving instructor Tara Hunter nearly lost everything in an accident that saw her medically discharged from the navy. With the help of the Warrior Fight Club, she's fought hard to overcome her fears and get back in the water where she's always felt most at home. At work, she's tough, serious, and doesn't tolerate distractions. Which is why finding her gorgeous one-night stand on her new dive team is such a problem.

Former navy deep-sea diver Jesse Anderson just can't seem to stop making mistakes—the latest being the hot-as-hell night he'd spent with his new partner. This job is his second chance, and Jesse knows he shouldn't mix business with pleasure. But spending every day with Tara's smart mouth and sexy curves makes her so damn hard to resist.

Joining a wounded warrior MMA training program seems like the perfect way to blow off steam—until Jesse finds that Tara belongs too. Now they're getting in deep and taking each other down day and night, and even though it breaks all the rules, their inescapable attraction might just be the only thing truly worth fighting for.

* * * *

Nothing Without You: A Forever Yours/Big Sky Novella
By Monica Murphy

From *New York Times* and *USA Today* bestselling author Monica Murphy…

Designing wedding cakes is Maisey Henderson's passion. She puts her heart and soul into every cake she makes, especially since she's such a believer in true love. But then Tucker McCloud rolls back into town, reminding her that love is a complete joke. The pro football player is the hottest thing to come out of Cunningham Falls—and the boy who broke Maisey's heart back in high school.

He claims he wants another chance. She says absolutely not. But Maisey's refusal is the ultimate challenge to Tucker. Life is a game, and Tucker's playing to win Maisey's heart—forever.

* * * *

All Stars Fall: A Seaside Pictures/Big Sky Novella
By Rachel Van Dyken

From *New York Times* and *USA Today* bestselling author Rachel Van Dyken…

She *left*.
Two words I can't really get out of my head.
She left *us*.
Three more words that make it that much worse.
Three being another word I can't seem to wrap my mind around.
Three kids under the age of six, and she left because she missed it. Because her dream had never been to have a family, no her dream had been to marry a rockstar and live the high life.

Moving my recording studio to Seaside Oregon seems like the best idea in the world right now especially since Seaside Oregon has turned into the place for celebrities to stay and raise families in between touring and producing. It would be lucrative to make the move, but I'm doing it for my kids because they need normal, they deserve normal. And me? Well, I just need a break and help, that too. I need a sitter and fast. Someone who won't flip me off when I ask them to sign an Iron Clad NDA, someone who won't sell our pictures to the press, and most of all? Someone who looks absolutely nothing like my ex-wife.

He's tall.
That was my first instinct when I saw the notorious Trevor Wood, drummer for the rock band Adrenaline, in the local coffee shop. He ordered a tall black coffee which made me smirk, and five minutes later I somehow agreed to interview for a nanny position. I couldn't help it; the smaller one had gum stuck in her hair while the eldest was standing on his feet and asking where babies came from. He looked so pathetic, so damn sexy and pathetic that rather than be star-struck, I took pity. I knew though; I knew the minute I signed that NDA, the minute our fingers brushed and my body became insanely aware of how close he was—I was in dangerous territory, I just didn't know how dangerous until it was too late. Until I fell for the star and realized that no matter how high they are in the sky—they're still human and fall just as hard.

* * * *

Hold On: A Play On/Big Sky Novella
By Samantha Young

From *New York Times* and *USA Today* bestselling author Samantha Young…

Autumn O'Dea has always tried to see the best in people while her big brother, Killian, has always tried to protect her from the worst. While their lonely upbringing made Killian a cynic, it isn't in Autumn's nature to be anything but warm and open. However, after a series of relationship disasters and the unsettling realization that she's drifting aimlessly through life, Autumn wonders if she's left herself too vulnerable to the world. Deciding some distance from the security blanket of her brother and an unmotivated life in Glasgow is exactly what she needs to find herself, Autumn takes up her friend's offer to stay at a ski resort in the snowy hills of Montana. Some guy-free alone time on Whitetail Mountain sounds just the thing to get to know herself better.

However, she wasn't counting on colliding into sexy Grayson King on the slopes. Autumn has never met anyone like Gray. Confident, smart, with a wicked sense of humor, he makes the men she dated seem like boys. Her attraction to him immediately puts her on the defense because being open-hearted in the past has only gotten it broken. Yet it becomes increasingly difficult to resist a man who is not only determined to seduce her, but adamant about helping her find her purpose in life and embrace the person she is. Autumn knows she shouldn't fall for Gray. It can only end badly. After all their lives are divided by an ocean and their inevitable separation is just another heart break away…

Discover 1001 Dark Nights Collection Six

DRAGON CLAIMED by Donna Grant
A Dark Kings Novella

ASHES TO INK by Carrie Ann Ryan
A Montgomery Ink: Colorado Springs Novella

ENSNARED by Elisabeth Naughton
An Eternal Guardians Novella

EVERMORE by Corinne Michaels
A Salvation Series Novella

VENGEANCE by Rebecca Zanetti
A Dark Protectors/Rebels Novella

ELI'S TRIUMPH by Joanna Wylde
A Reapers MC Novella

CIPHER by Larissa Ione
A Demonica Underworld Novella

RESCUING MACIE by Susan Stoker
A Delta Force Heroes Novella

ENCHANTED by Lexi Blake
A Masters and Mercenaries Novella

TAKE THE BRIDE by Carly Phillips
A Knight Brothers Novella

INDULGE ME by J. Kenner
A Stark Ever After Novella

THE KING by Jennifer L. Armentrout
A Wicked Novella

QUIET MAN by Kristen Ashley
A Dream Man Novella

ABANDON by Rachel Van Dyken
A Seaside Pictures Novella

THE OPEN DOOR by Laurelin Paige
A Found Duet Novella

CLOSER by Kylie Scott
A Stage Dive Novella

SOMETHING JUST LIKE THIS by Jennifer Probst
A Stay Novella

BLOOD NIGHT by Heather Graham
A Krewe of Hunters Novella

TWIST OF FATE by Jill Shalvis
A Heartbreaker Bay Novella

MORE THAN PLEASURE YOU by Shayla Black
A More Than Words Novella

WONDER WITH ME by Kristen Proby
A With Me In Seattle Novella

THE DARKEST ASSASSIN by Gena Showalter
A Lords of the Underworld Novella

Also from 1001 Dark Nights:
DAMIEN by J. Kenner
A Stark Novel

About Samantha Young

Samantha Young is the New York Times, USA Today and Wall Street Journal bestselling author of adult contemporary romances, including the On Dublin Street series and Hero, as well as the New Adult duology Into the Deep and Out of the Shallows. Fight or Flight, a new standalone published by Berkley Romance, released October 2018. Before turning to contemporary fiction, she wrote several young adult paranormal and fantasy series, including the amazon bestselling Tale of Lunarmorte trilogy. Samantha's YA contemporary novel The Impossible Vastness of Us and The Fragile Ordinary are published by Harlequin TEEN in ebook & hardback.

Samantha is currently published in 30 countries and is a #1 international bestselling author. When she's not writing books, she's buying shoes she doesn't really need and searching for nooks and crannies to shelve her ever-expanding book collection.

For more information visit https://authorsamanthayoung.com

Fight or Flight

By Samantha Young
Coming October 9, 2018

A series of chance encounters leads to a sizzling new romance from the New York Times bestselling author of the On Dublin Street series.

The universe is conspiring against Ava Breevort. As if flying back to Phoenix to bury a childhood friend wasn't hell enough, a cloud of volcanic ash traveling from overseas delayed her flight back home to Boston. Her last ditch attempt to salvage the trip was thwarted by an arrogant Scotsman, Caleb Scott, who steals a first class seat out from under her. Then over the course of their journey home, their antagonism somehow lands them in bed for the steamiest layover Ava's ever had. And that's all it was—until Caleb shows up on her doorstep.

When pure chance pulls Ava back into Caleb's orbit, he proposes they enjoy their physical connection while he's stranded in Boston. Ava agrees, knowing her heart's in no danger since a) she barely likes Caleb and b) his existence in her life is temporary. Not long thereafter Ava realizes she's made a terrible error because as it turns out Caleb Scott isn't quite so unlikeable after all. When his stay in Boston becomes permanent, Ava must decide whether to fight her feelings for him or give into them. But even if she does decide to risk her heart on Caleb, there is no guarantee her stubborn Scot will want to risk his heart on her....

* * * *

"I'd like tae upgrade tae first class, please," he said in a deep, loud, rumbling, very attractive accent that did nothing to soothe my annoyance with him for cutting in front of me.

"Of course, sir," the flight attendant answered in such a flirtatious tone I was sure that if I was tall enough to see over the big guy's shoulder I would see the flight attendant batting his lashes at him. "Okay, flight DL180 to Boston. You're in luck, Mr. Scott. We have one seat left in first class."

Oh hell no!

"What?" I shoved my way up next to rude guy, not even looking at him.

The flight attendant, sensing my tone, immediately narrowed his eyes on me and thinned his lips.

"I was coming here to ask for an upgrade on this flight and he," I gestured to my right, "cut in front of me. You saw him do it."

"Miss, I'm going to ask you to calm down and wait your turn. Although we have a very full flight today, I can put you on our list and if a first class seat opens up before the flight, we will let you know."

Yeah, because the way my week was going that was likely.

"I was first," I insisted, my skin flushing because my blood had turned so hot with anger at the unfairness. "He whacked me with his laptop bag pushing past me to cut in line."

"Can we just ignore this tiny, angry person and upgrade me now?" the deep accented voice said somewhere above my head to my right.

His condescension finally drew my gaze to him.

And everything suddenly made sense.

A modern day Viking towered over me, my attention drawing his from the flight attendant. His eyes were the most beautiful I'd ever seen. A piercing ice blue against the rugged tan of his skin, the irises like pale blue glass bright against the sun streaming in through the airport windows. His hair was dark blonde, short at the sides and longer on top. And even though he was not my type, I could admit his features were entirely masculine and attractive with his short, dark blonde beard. It wasn't so much a beard as a thick growth of stubble. He had a beautiful mouth, a thinner top lip but a full, sensual lower lip that gave him a broody, boyish pout at odds with his ruggedness. Gorgeous as his mouth may be, it was currently curled upwards at one corner in displeasure.

And did I mention he was built?

The offensive laptop bag was slung over a set of shoulders so broad they would have made a football coach weep with joy. I was guessing he was just a little over six feet, but his build made him look taller. I was only five foot three but I wore four inch stilettos, and yet, I felt like Tinkerbell next to this guy.

Tattoos I didn't take the time to study peeked out from under the rolled-up sleeve of his Henley shirt. A shirt that showed off the kind of muscle a guy didn't achieve without copious visits to the gym.

A fine male specimen, indeed.

I rolled my eyes and shot the flight attendant a knowing, annoyed look. "Really?" It was clear to me motorcycle-gang-member-Viking-dude was getting preferential treatment here.

"Miss, please don't make me call security."

My lips parted in shock. "Melodramatic much?"

"You." The belligerent rumble in the Viking's voice made me bristle.

I looked up at him.

He sneered. "Take a walk, wee yin."

Being deliberately obtuse I retorted, "I don't understand Scandinavian."

"I'm Scottish."

"Do I care?"

He muttered something unintelligible and turned to the flight attendant. "We done?"

The guy gave him a flirty smile and handed him his ticket and passport. "You're upgraded, Mr. Scott."

"Wait, what—" But the Viking had already taken back his passport and ticket and was striding away.

His long legs covered more ground than mine but I was motivated and I could run in my stilettos. So I did. With my carry-on bumping along on its wheels behind me.

"Wait a second!" I grabbed the man's arm and he swung around so fast I tottered.

Quickly, I regained balance and shrugged my suit jacket back into place as I grimaced. "You should do the right thing here and give me that seat." I didn't know why I was being so persistent. Maybe because I'd always been frustrated when I saw someone else endure an injustice. Or maybe I was just sick of being pushed around this week.

His expression was incredulous. "Are you kidding me with this?" I didn't even try not to take offense. Everything about this guy offended me.

"*You*," I gestured to him, saying the word slowly so his tiny brain could compute, "*Stole. My. Seat.*"

"*You.*" He pointed down at me, "*Are. A. Nutjob.*"

Appalled, I gasped. "One, that is not true. I am hangry. There is a difference. And two, that word is completely politically incorrect."

He stared off into the distance above my head for a moment,

seeming to gather himself. Or maybe just his patience. I think it was the latter because when he finally looked down at me with those startling eyes, he sighed. "Look, you would be almost funny if it weren't for the fact that you're completely unbalanced. And I'm not in the mood after having tae fly from Glasgow tae London and London tae Phoenix and Phoenix tae Boston instead of London tae Boston because my PA is a useless prat who clearly hasn't heard of international direct flights. So do us both a favor before I say or do something I'll regret… and walk. Away."

"You *don't* regret calling me a nutjob?"

His answer was to walk away.

I slumped in defeat, watching him stride off with the first-class ticket that should have been mine.

On behalf of 1001 Dark Nights,

Liz Berry and M.J. Rose would like to thank ~

Steve Berry
Doug Scofield
Kim Guidroz
Jillian Stein
InkSlinger PR
Dan Slater
Asha Hossain
Chris Graham
Fedora Chen
Kasi Alexander
Jessica Johns
Dylan Stockton
Richard Blake
and Simon Lipskar